Renato, a young railroad switchman, not a particularly religious person, suddenly finds, to his amazement and chagrin, that he is at times working miracles against his will and intention.

The scene of these extraordinary events is a small Spanish town in the grip of a merciless drought; and the story, as it unfolds with mounting suspense, shows the effects that Renato's miracles (and his reluctance to work them) have on the townspeople—good men and sinners, poor folk and mercenary worthies, frustrated women and plotting cynics, and the two priests of the stirred-up community. In a succession of swift-moving, dramatic scenes the novel moves toward its tragic climax—an inexorable ending that cannot fail to move the reader, whether he himself believes in twentieth-century miracles or not.

God's Frontier, a full-blooded novel reminiscent of the work of Georges Bernanos — and, thematically, also of Franz Werfel's *Song of Bernadette*—carries the reader forward not only on the swell of the narrative's plot and characterization, but also on the crest of the lucid, sinewy writing and its engrossing imagery.

Clearly, José Luis Martín Descalzo, a young Roman Catholic priest, is a novelist born.

GOD'S

FRONTIER

GOD'S FRONTIER

BY

JOSÉ LUIS MARTÍN DESCALZO

Translated from the Spanish by Harriet de Onís

ALFRED A. KNOPF / NEW YORK

1959

L. C. Catalog card number: 59–11746

© Alfred A. Knopf, Inc., 1959

THIS IS A BORZOI BOOK, *published by Alfred A. Knopf, Inc.*

FIRST AMERICAN EDITION

Originally published in Spanish as LA FRONTERA DE DIOS by Ediciones Destino, Barcelona, in 1957.

Dear Editor:

I cannot have peace of mind without writing these lines. I must say two things, and even though you may not print this letter, let me say them here.

The first has to do with my preoccupation over signing this novel as a priest. For many people, priestly literature and "edifying" literature are synonymous. And they would be if we had not ruined that marvelous word "edifying," if we realized that edification* is done with heavy blocks of stone and painful blows of the pick, and that it can be the work only of mature human beings. My novel is certainly constructive, but it has been made on this earth which, unhappily, is not "suitable for minors." Shall I be blamed if some of the pages of this work bleed or sizzle?

The second is to remind the reader that what he has in his hands is a novel, not a theological treatise or a sermon. Do not seek a thesis where it has tried to portray life; do not go looking for theological locutions when the characters are people who talk the way they talk. And remember, too, the ancient fact that the author does not always agree with every one of his characters, in this case not even those char-

---

* (Translator's note). In Spanish the word *edificación* has not lost, as it has in English, the meaning "act of building, of raising an edifice."

v

acters who are priests like himself. The priests of God's Frontier are not the Church; they are simply priests who live, suffer, die, and are resuscitated on high.

A third warning? Yes, for those who expect this novel to contain messianic insights. The problem of the Catholic novel is obscure enough, and perhaps someone thinks that he has the pattern: the Catholic novel will be one that resembles . . . Do not be ingenuous. When has a young man like myself pulled miracles out of his sleeve? Unhappily I am not Renato.

Well, let's have done. Would it be too much, my editorial friend, to ask you to put this letter at the beginning of my book?

Warmest greetings.

J. L. M. D.

GOD'S

FRONTIER

I

————

When Renato felt himself on the ground he lifted a hand to his forehead. He was completely bewildered. What were all those people kneeling there for? He rubbed his eyes to make sure that he was not dreaming. He was sweating. He took off his coat and handed it to someone, he didn't know whom.

"Go on, pray."

Renato turned his head in the direction from which the voices came, but he did not take in what they had said. It was as though they were talking to him from a distant land, in dreams.

"Pray."

"Me?" Renato asked, wiping his forehead with the back of his hand.

3

"Who else? That's what you came for."

It was then that Renato saw the broken-off cross, but he still was at a loss to know why all those people were kneeling there. He took a faltering step toward the cross.

"How dizzy I am," he said. And he felt a hand on his shoulder forcing him to his knees. He made no resistance, for he felt better when kneeling, more rested.

"What shall I pray?" he asked.

"Anything, whatever you want to."

Whereupon Renato, mechanically, as though repeating something he had done on many other occasions, shouted: "Lord, have mercy on us."

And he heard his words echo, like a surging tide: "Lord, have mercy on us."

He had to restrain himself from turning his head. "The whole village is here," he thought, "the whole town." But he went on: "Christ, have mercy on us."

Even louder, almost like a howl, the village repeated: "Christ, have mercy on us."

Once more Renato raised his hand to his head. His forehead and hair were soaking wet, and he felt as though a gigantic hand had been resting on him. It was then that he realized that a blazing sun was beating down unmercifully. His whole body was on fire. He shouted to God: "Why is this happening to me?" Miracles. It was stupid to ask miracles of God, to demand them. God knew full well when they should be worked. And him! Of all people, him! But he went on: "Send us rain."

"Rain, rain, rain."

"Have pity on our fields."

"Pity."

Renato was afraid as he was saying all this. Afraid of God, who might descend at any moment and crush them

4

all. Afraid of that wave roaring at his back, that village about to hurl itself upon him.

But suddenly he felt as though his heart was growing; he needed to talk. He turned his head and saw that the people were waiting for him to go on with that strange litany.

"Go on," said the curt voice of Don César beside him.

But now Renato paid no heed; he got clumsily to his feet—he had to rest the palm of his hand on the ground to steady himself—and turned toward the crowd. He looked one by one at the faces he had not recognized before. He saw the dense group of women which had opened up only a moment before to let him through; he saw the terrified faces of the children clutching their mothers' skirts; and the group of men leaning against the cemetery walls, and the boys rubbing their faces with their hands as they looked upon a scene none of them understood.

"Why have you brought me here?" he shouted. "What have I to do with your farces? God is going to crush us, any minute. Do you think you fool Him with your shouts? Can't you see that He is laughing at us? It is not with prayers that God is appeased, but with blood. You were able to throw the cross down, but you don't have the guts to raise it up. Where are the guilty ones? Right here among us, they are. Let them come forward. Come, you all know who they are, you could call their names. You are as foul as you were before. What good is it going to do you to call on God now?"

The sweat was dripping off Renato as he screamed these words. There was something almost grotesque about his gestures, and his eyes were starting from their sockets. The people hardly breathed as they listened to him, the

5

women watching him with fear while the children huddled still closer to their mothers.

"When you plowed your fields on Sunday you were not thinking about God. What kind of fruits do you expect them to bring forth now? God's curse has fallen on this town. What good is your shouting when the sin is here?"

Renato looked back at the cross as he said this. There it lay, the cross of the lake, fallen and broken into three pieces, the cross around which all the generations had gathered ever since Torre had existed. The cross of the pilgrimages, of the processions, the cross at whose foot all the newly baptized male children were laid so that God would make them strong and good farmers. That cross, the symbol of the fields, lay prone upon the ground. Renato looked at it, and all eyes were drawn to it, following his. And the whole village trembled, understanding.

"And you, what have you come for?" he cried, turning to Don César. "What for? Matilde didn't come with you, did she? Everybody knows where you spent the afternoon, and now you come here to pray like a woman. Your fields . . . I shit on your fields! What does God care about your cows? To hell with the lot of them. They won't wipe out, the whole herd of them, the filth you pile up in a single night."

Don César clenched his fists and his teeth, and the whole town waited to see him get up and then the two of them go rolling on the ground. But it did not happen. Don César, on his knees, felt himself humiliated and overpowered by Renato's eyes. He could not get over his amazement. He could not believe that this man who was upbraiding him now was the crossing switchman of half an hour before. Now he was a giant who held in his hands the fate of himself and the whole village. He barely had the courage to say: "Keep still!"

"Keep still? I will not keep still. I will not keep still, now that you have brought me here. You asked me to pray to God; now you'll have to put up with me. It's not so easy to keep still once you start talking. Why have you come here? You, Lucas, you, Martín, what is it you believe? You think you can play hide-and-seek with God? Pulling those mournful faces now! God knows you just the same. He knows your voices by heart from all your blasphemies. You might just as well know it. The vines will wither, the wheat will rot, and we shall die of hunger. Once we are dead there will be an end to sinning, and God will get some rest. The only reason you want rain for your vines is so that you can get drunk. Everyone knows where you go when you have money. And you—you were thinking about God when you did it, you sow.

"And now I'm to pray to God. Who do you think I am? I am nobody. None of us is going to halt the wrath of God. When your children are dying of hunger, then you'll remember God. What remains to be seen is whether He remembers you now."

Renato stopped, panting. Never in his whole life had he said so many words together. The whole village watched him, hardly breathing. No, this was not the crossing switchman they knew; it was as though he had suddenly grown. His voice had a strange tone of assurance, as of one who spoke with authority. That was why they kept silent under the merciless sun beating down on the plain.

The fields were burning up, motionless, without a whisper of air. The leaves of the trees that flanked the little road winding up to the hermitage were parched and yellow. There, by the dried-up lake, the fallen cross lent a tragic note to the scene. Above the dusty walls of the cemetery two dark cypresses raised their tips. Beyond it, the village throbbed in silence; from time to time there came the sound of the mournful lowing of the hungry cows.

Renato now moved nervously and looked upward as though quarreling with God. Suddenly he turned his head and shouted: "Now, everyone on their knees with me. We will call upon God morning and evening; we will spend the night here, and nobody will leave until God has taken pity on us. If anyone dies of hunger, let no one touch his body. Leave it there before God. We'll see if the stench reaches heaven. Let no one move from his place. And now all cry out with me. Until God hears us, whether He wants to or not."

At this a horrible clamor arose. Nobody knew exactly what he was saying. It was just a screaming. Perhaps they were saying nothing, and only fear moved their lips. The women uttered shrieks that frightened the children more and more, who clung to their skirts, weeping. Some of the men, caught up in the general fear, were screaming too; they wept like children, those men who two hours earlier had seemed fortresses. And none of them understood why. It was like a collective madness: the whole village screaming as though in the face of an earthquake or the direst catastrophe. The lowing of the cows in the stables had risen, too, and to this was added the barking of all the dogs of the town, which came rushing through the Calle de las Monjas, drawn by the screams.

The visible specter of hunger was marching through the fields under that maddening sun.

8

Several hours went by, but nobody moved. Now the clamor had become muted, and was only the murmur of "Our Fathers" and "Hail Marys," which rose and fell like waves, the one answering the other as though in a duel.

Renato, in front of the cross, clenched his hands and teeth. His face was burning. From his lips came an angry prayer, harsh, almost defiant. There was the cross, the huge stone cross, broken off almost even with its base, like an immense crime crying in the wilderness.

It was the tremendous symbol of all the sins of the village. The morning, a month before, when it had appeared broken-off, a shudder had run through the whole village. Nobody had asked questions, for they all had felt guilty. And the word spread that nobody had thrown it down, that it had fallen of itself, toppled by all the sins of the village.

Sito, the shepherd boy, had been the first to discover it. When he went out that April morning to the grazing grounds with his sheep, he found the cross on the ground. The boy felt as though a hand had clutched his heart; perhaps it was the memory of that afternoon when he, too, had been laid, new-born, at the foot of the cross while his father and mother had sung the traditional song of thanksgiving:

> *This son you gave us,*
> *Preserve him, Lord,*
> *Make him strong of body,*
> *Stout of heart,*
> *That when a man*
> *He be worthy to*
> *Sow the wheat*
> *Of my Redeemer's body.*

Perhaps this unconscious memory had made Sito approach the cross with fear and reverence and then, forgetting the sheep, run home as fast as he could.

"Father, they have thrown down the cross."

Maneras rushed out of his house, pulling on his coat as he ran, as though hurrying to a sick person who could still be helped. On the way the father asked: "Did you leave the sheep alone?"

Only then did Sito realize what he had done. "I was afraid," he answered.

The father said nothing. But he thought: "God will tend them."

When Nicolás and his son reached the cross, they found all the sheep huddled together between it and the cemetery, not even stirring. It did not enter Maneras's mind to count them; he was sure that they were all there. He stopped in front of the cross and stood looking at it as though some grave misfortune had fallen upon his house and the village. Sito would have liked his father to talk, to do something, but Nicolás stood, his feet apart, as though rooted to the ground, shaking his head sadly.

"Father," the boy began, but he did not go on with his question.

Finally Nicolás spoke: "What is done is done. May God forgive it. You go on with the sheep."

The boy nodded and went off down the road, lost in the cloud of dust the flock stirred up. Nicolás made his way back to the village slowly. He called at Uncle Lucas's house. "They've thrown down the cross," he said when the old man appeared in the doorway.

"The cross of the lake?"

"Yes, last night."

"God!"

The news had run from house to house, and all the inhabitants of the village had filed past the cross and had remained silent for a few minutes. It was Uncle Lucas who said: "Now it is clear why it doesn't rain this year."

And all had raised their eyes to the sky, understanding that sentence had been passed.

The phrase of Don Macario, the old priest, spoken from the bed where he had lain ill for months, had run through the town, too. Don Macario had shaken his head sadly and had said: "This village was bound to end like this."

And when the three hundred and forty-seven inhabitants of Torre learned what he had said, they had the feeling that their village had ceased to exist, forever.

After that the drought was accepted by all as something normal. The men scanned the sky, but with the conviction that they would not discern on the whole horizon a cloud that gave hope of rain.

Then came that business of Rosa, who, when she learned that the cross had fallen, was seized by an uncontrollable shaking and weeping. The fact that Don Melquíades did not leave her bedside for one moment was of no avail, for it seemed that Rosa had made up her mind to die. She got paler and thinner by the hour, and all day long one cry was on her lips: "The cross, the cross—they must raise the cross."

It was useless for her children to gather around her bed trying to calm her. It was useless for Julián to lie, telling her that it had been raised. She kept crying: "No, I see it, I see it fallen. Only a miracle can raise it up. If anyone touches that cross, he will die. It is an accursed cross."

1 1

Rosa's cries had been heard throughout the village, even though Martín had kept the doors and windows closed, and all had trembled when they heard her. The old woman went on for twelve days, crying out for them to raise the cross and that only a miracle could raise it. When the other women heard her, they crossed themselves quickly.

On the thirteenth day Rosa died. She died without Don Melquíades being able to diagnose what ailed her, without even fever. They could all see how she wasted away, as though her soul was leaving her body in those cries. Until the day when, opening her eyes until it seemed that they would burst from their sockets, and screaming: "I see it, I see it fallen; it is a curse! The devil has entered this village," she writhed convulsively, clenching the sheet between her teeth, and then became motionless forever.

Not one of her children ventured to touch her, and the eyes of all the men and women of the village retained the image of Rosa writhing in her bed, and on her lips the words: "It is a curse, a curse of the devil."

And when the next day she was being taken to the cemetery, as the mourners approached the end of the Calle de las Monjas, which debouches into the lake beside which the cross had stood, many of them hung back and disappeared down neighboring alleys. And the few who followed the candle-bearers kept their eyes fixed on the coffin as though fearful that Rosa might rise up to take one final look at the fallen cross. And two of the young men who were carrying the coffin on their shoulders agreed that as they passed the cross Rosa had moved and the corpse had become heavier.

For that reason nobody in the village was surprised

when one of those evenings the fourteen women who gathered each evening to say the rosary under the guidance of Lucio, the sacristan, decided to say it before the cross instead of in the church. Nor did it cause surprise that the number of women grew from day to day, and that occasionally a man joined them.

This was how the village began to develop an obsession about the cross, and the women to see it in their sleep and the men to call upon it as the most binding of oaths.

"Swear by the cross of the lake."

"I swear."

"It's a deal."

The new moon marked the beginning of summer, and the men realized that beyond the shadow of a doubt it was not going to rain. Each day the number going into the fields was fewer; most of them spent their time in the tavern playing cards without talking.

But along with fear came rebellion, and with it blasphemy.

"God, God! What difference can one more cross on the earth make to Him?"

The men trembled as they said it, but felt relieved after it was out. This was their revenge, a low revenge, as they knew well, but still a revenge.

"My wife spends the day praying."

"Praying, praying . . . to a God whom we should send to . . ."

They were ridiculous blasphemies, the blasphemies of an insolent child, and much of the time the blasphemers were not so far removed from faith as they thought.

Holy Week came. From Irola, the capital of the province, came a Redemptorist father, tall, gaunt, and withered, who for three days thundered against sin and talked of

13

hell in a voice that made the women weep and left the men silent. But Father Mendizábal had a disagreeable surprise when on Friday, after he had been in the confessional four hours, not a single man had appeared before the holy bar.

"Don't the men in this village make confession?" he asked Don Macario as he paced nervously up and down the parish study. The voice of the priest answered from the alcove, whose curtains had been drawn back. "Badly, but they do."

"Not one has shown up today."

Nor the next morning, and Father Mendizábal learned that the men had sworn that not one of them would make confession or take communion during Holy Week if God did not send rain.

That afternoon the good father pulled out his most lugubrious stops, but with the same results.

"This has never happened to me before," he said sadly in his final sermon. "God's hand will be heavy upon you. You have undertaken to carry out your own vengeance, and the rain has departed for good."

But that afternoon nobody came to confession either, and the priest went out for a walk to chew the cud of his failure. He was fed up, and he left for the station half an hour before train time. And it was there that he had the greatest satisfaction of those three days.

A man came up to him and said: "Father, I am the crossing switchman. I have not been able to come to your sermons these days. You see, they were at the time the trains go by. This afternoon I went to church to make confession and—you were not there. I'd like to do it right here, if I could."

It was Mariano, the station porter, who told in the tavern that night that he had seen Renato making confession in a corner of the waiting-room, and it was Uncle Lucas who hung his head and, after a long pull at his pipe, said: "Maybe we did wrong."

"We shouldn't have done it." This was Martín, Rosa's son. He was thinking about his mother.

There was a long silence in the tavern.

On Easter Monday Pedro said: "Nothing can save this year's harvest now."

To which Feliciano added: "What a year lies ahead of us!"

On Tuesday it was Juanote who said: "My wife does nothing but cry all day long. She says God can't forgive us."

On Wednesday, Sito said to his father: "What are the sheep going to eat this year?"

"God will say," Maneras answered.

"God will say!" Pilar screamed from the back room. "We're the ones who have to say. There is nothing for it but to pray."

On Thursday, Maneras repeated in the tavern: "There is nothing for it but to pray."

"Pray!" Santos, the cheese-maker's son, repeated, and was on the point of adding a blasphemy, but lacked the courage.

"We're not even good for praying," Uncle Lucas said, hanging his head while the pipe went out between his lips.

"But we've got to do something." This was Tired Juan.

"For instance?"

"I don't know. But something."

"Find somebody to pray for us."

"Somebody. Who?"

"The priest."

15

"He's sick in bed and . . . he wouldn't listen to us."

There was a long pause.

"Maybe Renato." The suggestion came from Mariano, the station porter.

Uncle Lucas slowly raised his head. "Renato?" he said.

The men looked at one another in silence.

"He won't want to come," Martín said.

"You can't tell."

"Renato . . ." Uncle Lucas repeated, and he lighted up his cold pipe.

After that things had happened very fast. Renato rejected Uncle Lucas's arguments, saying this was a matter for priests. But he had not been able to reject the arms of Martín and Julián, who had almost dragged him with them. Now he was there, between the cross and the village, between two opposing tides: that of God, hermetic and silent as a stone, and that of the village, demanding that he bring about the miracle.

Renato was afraid. He felt small and ridiculous praying for things he neither knew nor even understood. He had always kept away from the village, happy in his little shack by the railroad, watching the trains go by, always alone, going to the village only to buy what he needed.

He felt ridiculous before God, before that God to whom he had always talked without flattery and from whom he now found himself forced to ask a magniloquent gesture. The very word "miracle" frightened him; he found it too imposing. He was accustomed to associate it only with the name of Christ and the saints.

Nevertheless, he prayed. He had no stake in the rain. Whether it rained or did not rain, the trains would go by the way they always had. But he had seen the terror on

16

the faces of the women, and for that reason he was shouting out the Lord's Prayer, the "Thy will be done," with what was almost a gesture of rebellion. His eyes were fastened on those fallen stones, which seemed to crush the village beneath their weight.

How did it happen? How do the great, the unforgettable things happen, when they do? Afterwards Renato could not remember. It seemed to him that he heard a howling, followed by a tense, moving silence. He had the feeling that a child was crying. He opened his eyes wide, incredibly wide, unable to believe what he was seeing: the cross was rising. The two pieces on the ground were moving, coming together, beginning to rise through the air, to stand up. Slowly. Slowly. So that all could see. The cross was rising as though being pulled by invisible cables, going back into place. It was standing. It was God. It could be felt.

The sun went on beating down on the plain like a huge fire, but nobody minded the heat any longer. The plain was a shouting, a raw, howling madness. Nobody knew what he was screaming. A miracle! A miracle! Hurrah! Hurrah! Some of them started running to the village, entering the houses, the stables, crying out the news.

Renato felt arms around him, his body rolling over the heads, as though that wave had finally broken at his feet. It was a sea, it was a sea dragging him he knew not where.

Some of the women were clinging to the cross as though out of their minds; everybody wanted to touch it; they were fighting one another to reach it. Nobody thought that the cross might fall again, with all that pushing. It was the hand of God, and they all wanted to touch it.

Nobody called for serenity. Hours later, without understanding what had happened, the village was still as though drunk, stupefied.

◇◇◇◇◇◇◇◇◇◇◇◇

2 Renato gave his head a hard shake. He had the feeling that a tight band of iron was pressing on his forehead. It was cool. This was the only rise on the whole plain, and the wind swept it. He got to his feet and tried to walk toward the hermitage to take shelter there. He felt drained, exhausted, and it was an effort for him to reach it. He dropped on the cement bench that ran the length of the outside wall, rested his head against the stones of the wall, and felt better. He was not aware of how long he sat there, but later he remembered that he had heard the town-hall clock strike three.

It was a clear night, and the full moon whitened the plain, which spread in space before Renato's eyes. There, below his feet, the village was bathed in a pale, milky light. He could plainly see the houses huddled tightly together around the square, solid tower of the church.

From the Colina de las Angustias, the only hill for miles around, all the villages of the region could be seen by day, small and brown like Torre de Muza. Renato observed the pine-flanked road that descended from the hermitage to the village, short but steep; then the small huddle of some hundred houses, and at the end, the Los Setos road, which came out at the ruins of the ancient Moorish tower that had given the village its name. A little farther on, beside the railroad, the last trees hid his cottage.

Now Renato felt a strange tenderness for the village. He had always considered himself somewhat detached from all its inhabitants, but he knew that now they were much closer to his heart, though he did not understand why. And as he gazed at the cemetery, which lay to the left of the hill, he felt as though all the dead sleeping there were linked to him by bonds much stronger than those of flesh and blood. He, who did not know to whom he was linked by blood.

Only when his eyes rested upon the stone cross standing upright beside the dry lake did he recall what had happened that afternoon. His recollection was blurred, and his whole body ached as though someone had made use of it for strange purposes. He seemed to remember that after many embraces he had managed to escape from the people, that he had fallen twice climbing the Colina de las Angustias, but had got up quickly both times, as though aided by an invisible hand, perhaps fear.

Once on the hill, he had hidden in the pine grove and had heard the shouting moving off in the direction of the village. His body had felt heavy, and he had dropped to the ground among the trees. Now he seemed to recall something like having demanded an accounting of God. Then he had fallen asleep for several hours.

The church clock gave the two strokes of the half-hour. Renato felt tired, empty. But when he buried his head in his hands, this question came to him: why had all this happened to him? Miracles were not his business. Who had the right to upset his life like this? All he wanted was to live in peace, nothing else. Simply to live in peace. And now? Who could turn back the wave? Renato realized that this was not going to be the end, that that May 25 had destroyed his life for good, dividing it into two halves. What was to come after this he could not dream. But good-by to his happy life of throwing the switches and watching the trains pass. God—had God the right to do this?

It was nearly four o'clock when he began to descend the slope. He walked slowly, and with each step dislodged pebbles that rolled several yards ahead of him. Halfway down he stopped. He was afraid to go near the place that had changed the course of his life. He leaned against All Souls' tree, the biggest pine of the village, into which all who visited the hermitage drove a white pebble for each Lord's Prayer they said. Under the moon the tree had a magic phosphorescence.

Then Renato became aware of the fact that there was someone before the cross. He saw a kneeling shadow that raised and lowered its hands in gestures that were comical from a distance.

The crossing switchman approached slowly, hiding among the pines, to see who it was without being seen.

When he came near, he could make out the shadow of a man who, kneeling before the cross, was talking in a loud voice as he raised his hands heavenward. Then, in a strange movement, he saw the man touch the ground with his head, and it seemed to him that he heard weeping punctuated by sobs. Then he saw the shadow arise, approach the cross, and, finally, clasp it, still talking in a loud voice. But Renato could not understand what he said because the wind carried the sound off in the direction of the village.

He went nearer, now without the cover of the trees, but apparently the man did not see him, for he was still clasping the cross, his tears intermingled with groans. The switchman felt a kind of discomfort in his stomach, a feeling of contempt which he could not avoid. Then, when he was standing over the man, what he felt was nausea.

"You are not well today. You are cold. Cold. Cold. Love me, little one. Besides, it's going to rain, tomorrow it's going to rain. It was Renato, not me. Renato said: Come, arise, and it moved and . . . love me."

Renato roughly seized the hand that was clasping the cross. Then it let go, and Julián rolled to the ground without a sound.

"Come on, get up. And now go and sleep. It's high time."

"Yes, it is high time, yes. Thanks."

The switchman rested his hand on the cross. Once more his head was aching and he felt a strange urge to cry.

Then he saw another shadow kneeling beside the cemetery wall.

"Who's there?"

"Me. It's me."

It was a woman's voice. As he went closer, Renato could recognize the features of María, Don César's wife.

"What are you doing here?"

"I was praying."

"And did you see . . . ?"

"Yes. Julián. He's . . ."

"Does he do it often?"

"Yes. But today more. Many . . . are."

"Many?"

"Yes."

Renato did not venture to ask further questions. He was afraid of the answers. It was María who spoke: "The rejoicing wound up in the taverns."

Renato realized that he had not been mistaken when he had thought that the raising of the cross would not be the end of the affair. But he had to tell himself that this was something he had not foreseen.

"Many are still there. Drinking. My husband went . . . with . . ."

She gave a hopeless shrug and was unable to bring out the name.

"They say today is not a day to sleep, that the trouble is over. That tomorrow it will rain and it's something to celebrate."

She spoke in a low voice, with a sadness one could almost touch.

"It's dangerous to be out in the street tonight. A while ago Catalina was screaming because Santos was determined to go into her house while Uncle Lucas was sleeping off his jag. Then I saw them kissing each other."

"It's . . ." He could not find the adjective he was looking for.

Understanding him, she said: "It is."

Renato started off down the Calle de las Monjas. There was a light in Uncle Lucas's hayloft, the light of a lantern moving cautiously. From the street Uncle Lucas's snores were audible. From El Moro's tavern a slit of light and a stream of voices emerged. He saw two interlaced shadows come out and disappear, singing, and then they began pounding on the doors of the drugstore. Renato had not the heart to cross through the center of the village, and he turned down the Calleja de la Hoz toward the station.

The clock was striking four. The sky was flooded by a bright, round moon.

By half past four he reached the little station. It was deserted and the only light was shining in the station-master's room. Only then did the switchman remember his job and that the mixed freight and passenger train would be coming by at quarter to five.

Yes, Marcial had left. He had thrown the switch at seven and then he had left. Please God that he had done it right.

He walked around behind the building. (He knew the temper of Don Servando, the stationmaster, all too well.) And he hurried on, walking alongside the tracks. He would have to hurry if he wanted to be on time. It was hard for him to run with his body aching so.

He could see the trees around his house when he heard the train pull into the station. He thought to himself: "There's nobody there. They'll bring it right through. I should have told the stationmaster to hold it up a little." He quickened his pace, panting. He still had fifty yards to go when he heard the engine's whistle, which sounded shriller than ever in the silence of the night. He must hurry. Now his shoes hurt him. He pulled them off and went on running. The pebbles dug into the soles of his feet. "It's there," he thought, "it has arrived." But he hurried on. And then he saw that the little esplanade alongside his house was full of people.

"Here he is, here he is," several voices shouted while a dozen people ran toward him.

Renato stopped for a moment. He saw Manuela, who knelt down before him and clasped his knees, saying words that he could not understand. "Get out of the way," he said. "The train!" And he could hear the puffing of the

23

engine that was roaring up. He had to give the woman a shove that sent her sprawling on the ground because he heard the train at his back and she would not let go. He threw the switch seconds before the train entered the switch rail. He drew a deep breath and, resting on the lever, watched the train draw away and disappear into the depths of the night.

He was afraid to turn his head. He felt that all those people had come on some dirty business. He did not know what it was, but a strange fear seized him.

"Renato," a voice said at his back, "we have been waiting five hours for you."

It was Manuela, still covered with dust. She looked at him with an expression in her eyes which Renato found cloying.

"What were you waiting for?" he asked sourly.

"Come."

It was what he had feared. There were Uncle Juan, who had the ulcer, and Simona with her six-year-old son twisted by paralysis. And Alejandro the hunchback. And Luisa, from the store, on a divan. And Don César's lame daughter. And Doña Asunción, the mother of the butcher, who was always at death's door. And Delfín with only one leg. And Nano, the monkey boy. All of them with their relatives, and an escort of curiosity-seekers. In the distance the dogs kept up an incessant barking.

Suddenly Renato understood. He felt the blood rush to his head, and his lips tightened. "Idiots!" He said the word slowly, chewing the syllables. "What has come over you? Do you think God has nothing to do but listen to you? He is not a snake-charmer. He doesn't work miracle to show off."

"You could help them." It was Carmela, the twin in a gray dress who spoke.

"Help them? In what?"

"Cure them."

"And then what? To sin. To go on sinning more comfortably. Sure, you can rob better with two hands than with one. Is that what you want? There are more important things than being well."

"Renato, you don't mean to say"—Manuela had stepped closer to him, with an air of defiance—"that you don't intend to go on with the miracles."

"Go on with the miracles? Since when is that a profession?"

"If you can do them, what stands in your way?"

"But who ever told you that I work miracles?" By now Renato was shouting and waving his arms around like a windmill.

"Wasn't what you did last night a miracle?"

"I didn't do it."

"Then who did?"

"Him." Renato pointed toward the sky.

"But you prayed to Him."

"I prayed the best I could." He was on the point of saying a coarse word, but he refrained. "Prayers don't work miracles. They're God's doing. Or if not, go to the priest. Praying is his business. I am the crossing switchman. That's all."

"There's nothing to be lost by trying."

"Nothing, or everything. You don't fool around with God. And least of all, to fill our bellies."

"You have a heart of stone." Doña Asunción moaned. "And God will punish you."

"Do us this kindness."

25

"Shut up!"

"Be kind, Renato. Look, he's only six years old." Simona had stepped forward with her boy in her arms.

"Please go away. Why won't you understand me? I can't do this," he shouted. "And you even ought to be ashamed of yourselves to bring the children here. These are not the best lessons for them. Now you remember God. And if the devil worked miracles, you'd go running to him. And take your children."

It was then that María Belén stepped up to him. Her body would have been monstrous if it had not been for the light in her eyes. She was nine years old, and one of her legs was shorter than the other. This had gradually twisted her body to the left until her back was completely deformed. But her eyes were wonderfully luminous and gay. They were enough. "I didn't come here for you to heal me."

Her voice was almost as clear as her eyes. She paused for a moment. Distant on the horizon, the dawn was breaking. The lame girl took another step and her eyes gleamed in the light of the lamp shaking in Manuela's hand. Renato trembled as he looked into the clarity of those childish eyes.

"I did not come for this," she repeated, pointing to her dragging leg. She opened her hands and showed him a small dark object. Manuela brought the lamp near, and several of the people came close.

"What is it?"

"It looks like a bird."

The lame girl went on: "It died three days ago. Last night when I saw what you did, I thought . . . In the catechism it says that Jesus resurrected people. Birds are easier."

Renato became aware of the fact that it was growing lighter each minute. The dogs he had heard barking had fallen silent. The girl said: "How can I bury it again?"

Not a sound was heard among the people. Renato felt that weariness again, but with it a strange joy. It seemed to him as though his very blood was cooler now, as though suddenly he was seeing that sea again, lost in the memories of infancy.

The lame girl was watching him with eyes wide like pools.

Renato took the bird in his hand. "Was it a canary?" he asked.

"Yes. It sang. It sang all day long."

"Did you love it?"

"Oh!"

The wind had died down, and it was easier to breathe. Renato felt in his rough hand the dirt on the canary. He noticed, too, how soft its feathers were. He held it up to the lamp. Its head hung as though its neck was broken, and its eyes were filmed over. There was dried mud on its beak. He blew on its wings to remove the dirt. He began to stroke it.

"Will you make it well for me?" the child asked, as though it were a sick person.

"Miracles are only something extra. You understand? What matters is love. Being good, that's what matters."

"Belén was good. Her name was Belén," the child explained.

"Yes, Belén was good. She sang and was beautiful without knowing it. She gave everything to others, to you. Belén . . ."

Renato felt warmth between his palms, a warmth that was different, that was life, a throbbing of which he could not say whether it came from his own blood or from that of another.

Dawn's diffuse light was spreading across the plain as every eye was riveted on Renato's hands. He realized that something marvelous had happened, and he was afraid to open them to confirm it.

"You've cured it already. You've cured it for me already!"

"Here, take it. See that it doesn't ever die again."

The clock struck five. The sound was followed at once by the rumble of a train, and then the lights of the approaching express became visible. Everyone turned his head. The express did not stop at the village, but whizzed by like a flash of lightning. The girl was clinging to Renato's neck and kissing him.

"This is ridiculous," someone said after a pause.

"Absolutely ridiculous," Carmen agreed.

"And what about this miracle? This one." Manuela had stepped forward, in an attitude of defiance.

"This one . . ." Renato tried to explain, but he realized that there was nothing he could say.

"What trouble would it be for you to cure us?"

The switchman shook his head. "It's not that. You have to understand that I can't, no. . . ."

"You don't want to. There's the canary."

"That . . ."

The girl had remained beside him, with his arm around her, as though to protect herself. She watched the people with a frightened air.

"This is . . ." Renato went on.

"Miracles like this are stupid." It was Manuela speaking. Once more Renato had the feeling that he was awaking

28

from a dream. He could not understand how a miracle could be called stupid, no matter what kind it was.

"It makes God look foolish," affirmed Carmela, the twin dressed in gray.

"Making Him waste His time on nonsense. As though there weren't enough canaries in the world," said the one dressed in blue.

"You ought to cure him for me, Renato. He's my only child, you understand."

Renato looked toward Pedrín. He saw the childish body, so strangely twisted; he saw the stupid expression in the eyes staring off into space. He felt his heart beating faster.

There came another gust of the cool morning breeze, and the light beyond the horizon was growing stronger by the minute.

Renato shook his head as though to drive off temptation. "No, no, I can't."

Simona burst into tears. "God will punish you. You are not good."

"I . . . I . . ." Renato began. He would have liked to say that the thing he wanted most was to cure them all, but that that was God's affair. But he did not know how. All he said was: "God is God. . . ."

"God! God!" Uncle Juan shouted.

The lame girl pressed closer to Renato.

"We don't give a hoot about your God. Do you understand?"

The girl turned her head toward the old man. "That's blasphemy."

Uncle Juan laughed. "You little fool! You think bringing a canary back to life is something so wonderful?"

"He thinks about us. More than we about Him."

Renato looked down at the girl, asking himself where she found these words.

She went on talking: "We ought to be wild with joy."

"Don't be a foolish child." It was Uncle Juan again. "Why should we be wild with joy?"

"God has come."

"God has come. And what? Your leg and my stomach are the same as before."

"What does my leg matter?"

"Splendid!" The old man laughed. "In four days tell me which would have been better: to cure your leg or perform this foolishness with a bird."

Uncle Juan now turned toward Renato, a scowl on his forehead. "As for you, you clown, go to hell with your miracles."

He had started to leave, but turned back. "And you should know that you're on a dangerous road. Don't forget that I warned you."

It was broad daylight when Renato dropped onto his bed. He would have liked to sort out the happenings of the last hours, but everything was churning about in his head: "Love me, love me, darling. The train; I must get there; if I'm late something terrible will happen. Come on, pray. Hooray! Hooray! You're on a dangerous road. I'm warning you. Why does this have to happen to me? Bringing canaries back to life is silly. God has been among us."

He turned restlessly in the bed. "What is going to become of me now?" He would have to lock himself up. Lock himself in his house and never go out again. Never.

At that moment he heard a knock at the door. He was

afraid. Again! He tried to get up and slide the bolt home. The knocking went on. He was too tired to get up.

"Come in."

The door creaked. It was María Belén. Renato breathed.

The child said: "It's me." She held out her hand with a package wrapped in newspaper. "I went and got the cage. I'm giving it to you." She became sad for a moment, and then smiled. "You'll let me see it sometimes." Her voice failed her. She set the cage on the floor and started toward the door. Turning back, she said: "And I wanted to thank you, too."

◆◆◆◆◆◆◆◆◆◆

3   If all these things had not happened, nobody would have recalled Renato's past, a past that was fading into forgetfulness but sprang up afresh on the lips of all the inhabitants of Torre that night. And there were expressions of amazement on the faces of those who heard it for the first time.

Renato had not been born in the village. Some twenty years before, he had arrived in a covered wagon with a group of circus performers. He was about seven at the time, and with him were a man and two women. The man was short and slightly cross-eyed, and he played the clown and recited sentimental ballads. The boy juggled six balls and was the delight of the young and the women in the audience. The two women's only visible attraction

3 1

was the amount of skin they displayed in their dances. As a matter of fact, their performance was only a come-on for the village lads who returned to the wagon after dark. What the relationship among the four players was, nobody knew. Whether the man was the husband of one of them, and, if so, which; whether the child belonged to one of the women, or had been stolen from some village, it was impossible to find out. Perhaps this atmosphere of mystery and scandal contributed to the success of the show.

They stayed in Torre for three days. And their stay wound up in tragedy. Perhaps things did not go well with them in the village; perhaps it all began with an argument, or the man had drunk too much. At any rate, the following day, on hearing sobbing in the wagon, and when no one had shown up by midmorning, the villagers opened the door, and found the two women, half dressed, strangled with a necktie and a pair of stockings. In a corner the child was crying inconsolably. The man had disappeared. The police were notified, and they caught up with him in a tavern in Irola. He defended himself with a pistol, and fell dead across the table, riddled with bullets.

This had been Renato's entrance into the life of Torre. It is true that a wave of sympathy reached out from every house toward the child, but it is also true that every heart was constrained by that bitter judgment men pass on those over whose cradle a shadow lies. As a result, although everyone in Torre would have liked to see the child playing in its streets, at the same time they were unanimously impatient for him to leave the village as quickly as possible.

And this would have happened except that after all arrangements had been made to put him in the orphanage of Irola, Don Serafín, the stationmaster, had stepped into the picture.

Don Serafín was corpulent, and his shining baldness crowned a head as large as it was full of strange notions. He was married to Doña Petra (who was known to all, with that gift villages have for nicknames, as Doña Conejo, for never had a woman who looked more like a rabbit walked the earth), and they lived absolutely alone. In addition to living two kilometers out of the village, he was the stationmaster of a station on a practically dead line, and lived in a house that was a dead end. Doña Conejo had been able to give him neither children nor company. He liked to make jokes and bellow with laughter. She lived in a state of perpetual timorousness, as though in momentary fear that someone was going to strike her, and when she spoke it was as though she was apologizing for being alive. Nobody could understand what had made these two people, as different as day from night, fall in love, but life is full of such mysteries.

In spite of the planetary solitude in which Don Serafín lived, his decision to take the child into his house surprised nobody. When he informed Doña Conejo, she turned white, yellow, green, and finally red, and spent the day sniffling in the corners as though some major calamity was about to befall her. But she did not utter a word of protest. And Renato became the third pivot of that strange family.

Utterly devoid of possessions, Renato did not even have a name to take with him to Don Serafín's house. Although all the drawers and trunks of the wagon were turned out, nothing could be learned of the child's origins, and Don Macario, the priest, proposed, just to be on the safe side, that he baptize him *sub conditione*, lest the town harbor a young infidel. The entire village turned out for the ceremony, for this was the first time the baptismal waters had been poured on a child who walked up to the font under his own power. It occurred to Don Serafín, to give the act a certain symbolism, to have the child named Renato—"reborn"—inasmuch as Chico, which was what the players called him, did not seem exactly a Christian name. And when, after the baptism, the village saw the neophyte scrambling on the ground with the other children for the candy the godfather tossed out, all felt a strange happiness. They had accomplished what they wanted: the child remained in the village, though at a distance of two kilometers, which was sufficient to purify the air of his questionable origins. At heart they were proud of having Renato among them. His history was a small monument of local folklore with which to regale visitors.

The faint recollections of his earlier life gradually faded from the boy's mind, and years later all that remained was a remote memory of the sea, of having spent hours on end looking at it. Now it was the trains. For Renato was a child with a rare gift of abstraction. The least sight— the passing of the trains, the landscape, an anthill—could absorb his attention for hours. At such moments he opened his large dark eyes wide and remained motionless, as though missing a single detail was a question of life or death for him. If somebody called him, he did not hear, and if someone touched him on the shoulder, he started, and opened and closed his eyes as though returning from a strange land. This gave Doña Conejo her bad moments. When she called him and the boy did not answer, she was seized by the fear that he might have died, and when this happened she did not know whether to rush to him or call for help, and her throat went dry and her hands stiff. She would approach him on tiptoe, and only when she heard him breathing could she draw her breath. All this was not because she loved the child, but because it horrified her to think that someone might die in her house.

Renato's arrival changed Don Serafín's life. He took the boy into his office and there, hour after hour, read him the verses he had never dared to show anyone. The boy would sit looking at him, but off in his own world, so that he did not even hear what Don Serafín was reading. The stationmaster would break off to ask: "Do you like it?"

"Yes."

"Did you understand it?"

"No."

"What were you thinking about?"

"I don't know."

"You must have been thinking about something."

"You said one very pretty word."

"One word?"

"Yes: 'butterfly.' Don't you like it?"

A disconcerted expression came over Don Serafín's face, and he sent him out to play. Renato's favorite spot was the little garden beside the station. He would sit down beside an anthill and spend hours there.

"But why don't you play?" Don Serafín called from the window.

"I am playing." And he laughed.

Because Renato was always laughing, as though a minute without a smile was a minute lost. Always, when he was not woolgathering. Don Serafín said that he had two souls, which revealed themselves in his two only expressions: one when he laughed, which was his expression when he was with other people, and the other, devoid of meaning, which might have been that of a madman or a saint. In all other aspects the boy was nothing out of the ordinary. When he started going to school his grades were always average except in religion, in which they were high, but this was because the priest considered him a devout child as a result of that ability of his to spend hours looking at the altarpiece without blinking.

When Renato was ten years old, Don Serafín—who little by little had grown fond of the boy—decided to send him to a boarding school to complete his education. When he informed Renato, the boy frowned—it was the first time the stationmaster had ever seen this expression—and answered simply: "No."

"Then what are you going to be when you grow up?"

Don Serafín's eyes opened like saucers when the boy replied with complete assurance: "Switchman."

Only when he learned of the friendship that had grown up between the boy and the old switchman of Torre, Uncle Sopas, did he understand the reason.

Uncle Sopas was a small, withered old man who had been the switchman of Torre for nearly sixty years. He had been married twice, and had had nine children, but they had all died. Now he was alone, like the last leaf of a tree, ready to flutter down.

He and the boy had become friends one afternoon when he had found Renato leaning over an anthill and had told him about the life of the ants. Since that day the boy had gone to see him every afternoon, and the old man told him over and over again old stories and episodes of the African war. The child opened his eyes wide and listened without blinking, the same as when he watched an anthill.

One afternoon the boy unexpectedly asked: "Uncle Sopas, when you die, who will send the trains through?"

Uncle Sopas looked at him for a long time with an expression in his eyes the boy had never seen. Then he sighed and said: "Son, never ask old people questions like that."

This disturbed the boy. And after thinking it over for a long time he came to the conclusion that Uncle Sopas was afraid that when he died nobody would know how to signal the trains through and they would collide. The next day he interrupted him halfway through his story to say: "Uncle Sopas, don't you worry about the trains. I'll send them through when you die."

And Renato decided that this had pleased the old man, for he ran his hand over the boy's head several times while he shook his own from side to side. From then on the boy always went with the old man when he changed the points and watched him while he did it in the same way he would have watched a legendary hero display his greatest prowess.

All went along in this fashion until one day, when the boy was fourteen, Don Serafín woke up one morning with a severe pain in his side. Doña Petra was terrified and sent the boy for Don Melquíades. But Renato's race was for nothing, because when he got back with the doctor Don Serafín had been dead for half an hour.

Doña Conejo wandered about the house like an uneasy spirit for two days. Then Renato saw her gathering up her belongings, which two men loaded on a wagon. And it was only when, half an hour before the express was due, she gave him a kiss without saying a word, that he understood that she was leaving him alone.

But he did not feel abandoned. Without hesitating for a moment, he went to look for Uncle Sopas. And it was only when he found Uncle Sopas, too, cold and motionless across his bed that he felt really alone. He cried. But when he heard the sound of the approaching express, he felt as though someone inside him was tugging at him, and he rushed out and changed the points. When the train had passed, Renato realized that Uncle Sopas's death had been simply the last loving bequest of a fond grandfather: leaving him the job.

And when the new stationmaster learned that Renato's timely throwing of the switch left untended by Uncle Sopas's death had averted a bad accident, he recommended to the head office that he be given the job of switchman, in spite of the fact that he was only a boy. This was how Renato became the switchman of Torre.

Aside from this, nothing about his life was worth the telling. Just another boy, a little crazy and definitely odd, in the village opinion. He rarely came down, but usually spent the day at the door of his house. He whittled spoons out of wood, which the honey-vender sold in the city, and that was all he did. He had less and less to do with people; at first they prepared his food in the house of the new stationmaster and he carried it home in a saucepan, but he wound up cooking it himself.

The village gossiped about his ways, calling them quirks. By the time he was nineteen, he was a good-looking lad, and there was no lack of girls who, on one pretext or another, always had something to do along the road that led to the switchman's house. But Renato never seemed to know what they were up to. He would talk with them, and then suddenly he would be off at his woolgathering. Their flow of conversation dried up and they went off discouraged. "He lives in the moon," they would say.

His complete indifference to money was another topic of conversation. When he did his shopping in the village, he always paid the asking price, even though it was three times the normal charge. And he never counted his change. The shopkeepers sometimes amused themselves by short-changing him, but he never realized it, and they would make it up the next time, giving him more, which he did not notice either. Perhaps this indifference was the reason nobody ever ventured to cheat him.

But by now even this aroused no comment. Everybody knew about it, and it surprised no one. Renato was just one more among Torre's population of 347. He was now about thirty. He was strong, not very tall, and heavy-shouldered. His eyes were defiantly black, and often underwent a curious change: either they were so alive that they were the center of his personality, or they remained opaque, lost among his other features. His hair was black and very thick (he never remembered to have it cut), and often fell over his forehead. Perhaps this was the reason for his habit of running his hand over his brow to push it back. He was a little hard of hearing, and always talked too loud. But it was not easy to understand him, for he talked in spurts, and all his phrases began clumsily and haltingly, to end in a rush of words. The truth of the matter is that few of the villagers had heard him talk. Perhaps only the children. Every day, toward evening, a group of young ones went scampering down the road to

39

Los Setos. And Renato would sit with them on the ground and tell them about the life of the ants and stories of the African war.

And always at the end: "Now the balls; do the balls for us."

And Renato would juggle six balls, faster and faster.

◇◇◇◇◇◇◇◇◇◇◇

4 "Well?" Don Macario smiled behind his horn-rimmed spectacles.

Don José Antonio stopped. He pursed his lips like a funnel and let out a long puff of smoke.

"Marvelous," he said. "A full house, absolutely full. I haven't got over my surprise."

Don José Antonio paced up and down Don Macario's study, while the latter lay half-reclining in his bedroom, which communicated with the study by means of a wide glass door with papered panes.

Don Macario was sixty-four and had been the priest of Torre de Muza for thirty years. His face was not that of an old man, but of one who had suffered. The wrinkles were deep furrows, and the folds were like those of a crumpled ball of paper. His eyes were deep-set, restless, and wise. There were times when they were clouded over as by a great fear. He was skin and bones after six months in bed almost without eating.

Don José Antonio was tall and thin. His chin was sharp and so was his nose. Only his eyes betrayed his personality; behind glasses like those of President Truman, they showed dull and timid. "Deer eyes," someone in San Martín had said on his arrival there. For he was not the priest of Torre, but of San Martín del Río, four kilometers away. But he had been ordered to care for the faithful of Torre since Don Macario's sickness, and every Sunday he came and went from one village to the other by bicycle, always covered with the dust of the infernal roads. There was a touch of pride in his air, that air typical of the meek who suddenly feel themselves in command of a situation. But this could not quite conceal a kind of fear, as of one who expects to step into a trap at any moment. He talked with a faint stammer, hardly more than a hesitancy, which gave him away. "Marvelous," he repeated.

"Usual, my son, the normal thing." Don Macario stirred in his bed. "In these villages curiosity is always stronger than religion."

"That's true. What can't be accomplished in a year's preaching happens in one day with a . . ."

"With a what?"

"Miracle, I was going to say. But . . ."

"And what has your theology to say about this?"

"I don't know. But if you want me to be completely sincere, I don't care for miracles. Please God that they don't bring the village problems."

"That's impossible, son. I cannot say whether this is a miracle or a case of collective hysteria. What I can tell you is that it would be easier all around if it were hysteria. Miracles are very troublesome things."

"Are you joking?"

"No, son, I'm giving you my honest opinion. A miracle is a dangerous luxury. Everything is going along fine, without complications, without problems . . . until God

41

takes it into His head to draw near men. Heaven help those whom God approaches! It is a dangerous business. He is like the sun, which we like because we are far enough from it so it doesn't burn us."

"But the saints . . ."

"You are only proving what I say: the saints entered the danger zone, and it cost them dear. We're not the timber saints are made of, son, not me anyway. I belong to the race of cowards."

He hesitated for a moment, smoothing the spread. Then he went on: "One becomes a priest, dreaming of sanctity, and then one finds he has become a comfort-loving bourgeois. One even gets the impression that our vocation is exactly that: to be good, bourgeois, perfect white-collar workers who neatly pack up souls for heaven. Sanctity is a risky thing, son."

"But Christ . . ."

"Son, never forget that phrase of the Scriptures: 'He will bring ruin and salvation to many.' And notice that ruin is put first. Yes, it is really a good thing Christ is not here among us. It would be terrible if He were to look us in the eye even if only once a year."

He sighed and smiled as he observed the expression on Don José Antonio's face. Then went on: "Of course, I realize that all this surprises you. This is not what your spiritual adviser said to you in the seminary. But if we were all sincere, we would confess that we could not stand Christ as a neighbor. Oh, yes, in heaven it will be another story. I know it. At any rate, I hope so. But heaven and earth are two very different propositions. Look, maybe if Judas had been dealing with us and not with Christ, things would have worked out in the end. Today he would be a banker and sleek, not gaunt and sallow as he is painted. And what a 'Christian' obituary the papers would have carried when he passed on!" He stirred in his bed. 'Raise this pillow a little. There, that's fine. Thanks. I get tired of the same position. Besides, I like it better sitting up. I'll have plenty of time to be stretched out in the coffin."

Don José Antonio looked at Don Macario without wholly understanding him. It had always been like this. He had never known whether Don Macario was crazy or what. Certainly, he spoke from a different world than his own, and the young priest was never sure whether his words were profound experiences or simply heresies. No, the cassock had not made them alike.

Don Macario laughed. "This problem is made to order for you."

"For me?"

"Yes, you can't file God and miracles in your card indexes."

The young priest turned his head sharply, but did not answer.

"Nor in your statistics," Don Macario went on. Then he stopped, with an ironic gleam in his eyes, and asked: "Tell me, how had you classified Renato?"

Don José Antonio hesitated, flushed, and said: "In the middle group."

"There you are. And then God comes along and takes one of your lukewarm to work the miracles."

The young priest did not answer. He realized that Don Macario had struck home. He was thinking about his first meeting with the old priest.

"If you want a word of advice, here it is. Limit yourself to your Masses, marriages, and baptisms. Preach, but make your sermons short and simple. Don't attack anyone. That is your best course with these people. Listen to me: those who want to go to heaven, go by themselves. And those who don't, go to hell without even thinking about it. I've been here for forty years, and I can't recall a single instance of a so-called conversion."

Don José Antonio had not ventured to protest on that occasion. But several Sundays later he had spoken in the church about certain new organizations. That day, as he was having breakfast, Don Macario sent for him.

"Look, son, I know it is not your fault. There in the seminary they stuffed your heads with ideas. But you might as well face it: it's all nonsense. No, I'm not forbidding you. I could because I am still the priest of this village. But I'm not going to do it. Nevertheless, let me repeat my advice: if you want to be happy, keep out of brier patches."

"But it's not a question of being happy or not. It's a question of saving them."

"No, son, it's a question of letting them save themselves. It's not the same thing."

This distinction had not convinced Don José Antonio, who had gone on tilling his vineyard and even felt satisfied. The societies were flourishing; more children were studying the catechism. And one day he decided to make a graph. He recalled his classes in religious sociology at the seminary. He made a big chart representing the parish, showing three concentric circles. In the first he put the names of the faithful, nearly all feminine. The second and largest listed the good. And the third—large too—was occupied by the "indifferent."

When Don José Antonio had been vain enough to show it to him, Don Macario had laughed heartily and had read out the names one by one, underscoring each with laughter more or less prolonged. Then he had said: "All right, son. Amuse yourself with this if you find it fun. But don't get your hopes up. When one of the middle circle goes over to the faithful, be sure to let me know. It will call for a celebration. With firecrackers. Not the backslidings; we won't celebrate those. There would be too many." Then he went on, in serious vein: "As for me, I can assure you that . . ."

"That what?"

"That I would not have dared. No, I would not have dared to do this, never."

"But why?"

"It's like getting the jump on God. I have a feeling that on the Judgment Day you are going to be in for an awful lot of surprises."

Don José Antonio was remembering that conversation. He said to himself: "The first surprise." But he could not accept such a mistake: Renato was in the middle area, and now he was working miracles. And Don José Antonio doubted the miracles because he could not doubt his statistics. When he had heard about it the day before in San Martín, he had not for a second believed that it was true. But the full church had impressed him. He told himself: "By their fruits ye shall know them." And a full church was the best fruit he could imagine.

He was pacing the parochial study nervously. It was a large, low-ceilinged room, and in the middle of it there was a huge table. Behind this a built-in bookcase in which the parish books were kept covered a whole wall. Don Macario's own books—they were many—stood dusty in another bookcase against the opposite wall.

"I have made up my mind not to read any more," he used to say. "I think I have told you that when Abderraman burned the library of Damascus, he was the smartest man the world has ever known. 'Either all this is in the Koran, and in that case, I have enough with the Koran; or it says the contrary, and in that case it is harmful.' That's not bad. Six hundred thousand volumes. God, what a fine bonfire they must have made."

Nevertheless, Don Macario had not yet been able to bring himself to burn his books, which stood pompously aligned on the shelves.

Don José Antonio had taken down a volume of sermons, thinking as he did so: "Good heavens, is it possible that he isn't going to talk about the matter?" This had been worrying him ever since he learned about the miracles. He made up his mind. "Don Macario . . ."

"What is it, son?"

"Don't you think that perhaps . . . it would be a good thing to report . . ."

"Report?"

"Report the matter . . . to the Palace?"

"Are you in earnest?" Don Macario now looked at him gravely, almost as though troubled. "That is the last thing, son, the last thing to be done. Haven't we got enough problems with God without getting the Bishop into it, too?"

The young priest's brow furrowed.

"No, not that," Don Macario said, putting an end to the matter. "I forbid you to do it. I am still the priest of Torre."

Just then Marta came into the room. "Don José Antonio, Manuela is asking for you."

"Tell her to come in."

"Isn't there a meeting of the circle today?"

"Yes, I'm just going," Don José Antonio answered.

He had a feeling of release when he came out into the plaza.

"Are we all here? Lucio, close the door." Sátrapa (that was Don César's nickname) spoke with authority, his voice like the bellow of a bull. "Let's sit down," he added.

There were six of them: Don Sebastián, the mayor; Don Melquíades, the doctor; Don Ricardo, the druggist; Uncle Lucas; Lucio, the sacristan; and Don César.

"Talk," Don César said.

Don Sebastián coughed. He was tall and thin, and his hair was cut close. He wore a coat that was too big for him, and his voice, in keeping with his figure, was thin and weak. In the village nobody knew him by his name; he was "Coughy," for he could not bring out three words together without first coughing several times. He was not only the mayor, but also the village schoolteacher. In the schoolroom he spent the day scolding and rapping the table with his knuckles without ever achieving quiet. No sooner was he seated at his desk than a symphony of coughs started up, for the worst of it was that the children, who began their mocking as a joke, ended up by really catching cold or, at any rate, the habit of coughing. To the point at which Don Melquíades became worried about the future of Torre: a village of consumptives.

"Coughy" coughed twice before beginning. "As Don César here has rightly said [as a matter of fact, Don César had not yet said a word], we are confronted with a difficult situation. This miracle . . ."

"Let's not use that word."

"Of course, Don César." He coughed twice. "It . . . what . . . has happened in this village creates, as I said, a difficult situation; a situation . . . difficult, that's it, difficult. And if one stops to think that really, that is to say, at a moment when one comes face to face with reality, that is when the real . . . the real value of those who are of value stands out. If one stops to think . . . for really men are not made for situations, but situations for men." He paused a moment, marveling at his own cleverness. He coughed.

Don César interrupted. "One thing is certain. It hasn't rained."

"That's right, it hasn't rained," Uncle Lucas repeated. "We hoped that the raising of the cross and the coming of the rains would be one and the same thing. But the cross has been up for almost a whole day, and . . ."

"This has been a cheat," Don Ricardo said with a touch of irony.

"A cheat."

"That's right, a cheat." It was Sátrapa who spoke. "The truth of the matter is that we put on too much of an act with that cross. All that praying before it, and God wasn't the least bit impressed. It hasn't done one bit of good."

Don Sebastián stirred in his chair, and twisted the ends of his mustache, thinking of what his wife would say if she had been listening. But he kept quiet. Then he went on: "Yes, the truth is that Renato played us a fine trick."

"There's only one thing to do," Lucio said, "and that is to get him to go on working miracles."

Don César interrupted: "That word again." Then in a calmer tone: "What does Father Macario have to say?"

"He doesn't want to hear about it. I spent two hours with him yesterday telling him all the details. He listened to the whole thing and didn't open his lips."

"Maybe Don José Antonio . . ."

"That young one." It was Sátrapa. "I don't care too much for him. But . . ."

The air by now was thick with smoke.

"Then what shall we do?"

"We could send for the switchman."

"That's making too much of him. That would be to make too much of him."

"How about a committee?"

"Worse."

"Suppose the young priest went?"

"You think he'd be willing?"

"Maybe with me." This was Lucio. "We can feel him out."

"All right. You handle it. And you know: the important thing is rain. We have to get that some way. And you can tell the priest that if it rains, the candles for the whole year are on me."

Uncle Lucas related Renato's history in the tavern. The place was more crowded than ever, and El Moro's eyes glittered behind the bar.

"It's a strange story. You were nothing but kids when it happened. He was just a little shaver when he came here. They were traveling in a wagon painted red and yellow. I can still see it. The man was one of those who can make you laugh as easily as he can make you cry. The women were two eye-fillers. They went play-acting through the villages, and then at night . . ."

"What about the man?"

"He didn't interfere."

"Was he the husband?"

"Nobody knew. Then one night he did them in. That you know."

49

"And what happened to him?"

"They shot him up in a tavern in Irola."

"And Renato?"

"He went to live with the stationmaster."

"Didn't he have any family?"

"Nobody ever knew."

"Maybe he was the son of one of those trollops."

"Or stolen."

"From another like her."

"Or some duchess."

"Or some duchess, who knows?" several repeated, inclined to take the romantic viewpoint.

"All I've got to say is that it hasn't rained," Pedrote suddenly shouted from the bar, waving his arms around like a windmill.

"That's a fact, it hasn't rained."

"What did I say?" It was Santos, who got up and moved over to Uncle Lucas's table. Bringing his fist down on it, he repeated: "Just what I said. That Matilde is a sow. I always said so. A filthy pig, as I always said."

"We all know what you have always said. That will do from you. Here, you hulk, take a drink." This was Martín, who led him away to a corner. "Here you can shoot off your mouth all you like."

The clock struck noon. It was a sunny day, and the excitement in the tavern mounted by the minute. On the radio Matachín, the singer in fashion at the moment, was squealing a *bayó*. One of the men began to accompany him with the motions of the dance.

"A fine time to be making sport," Uncle Lucas growled.

Someone shouted: "We ought to bring him here. We'll tank him up and he'll work all the miracles we want."

Uncle Lucas went on grumbling in his corner. "I can't figure out what there is to joke about," he said, and took a long pull at his pipe.

All the women in the first section of Don José Antonio's graph were at the circle meeting: Elena, the mayor's wife, tall, withered, with the yellowish skin of those suffering from epilepsy. Manuela, the wife of the sacristan, physically at the opposite pole from Elena; her bulk imposed respect. She always talked at the top of her lungs, and as she did so her flesh quivered as though her heart was trying to escape her body. The two "wee ones," Carmen and Carmela, whose nicknames came from the fact that they were nearly six feet tall, only a few inches shorter than their brother Don Melquíades. They were dressed in blue and gray, that being their mother's custom of dressing them so that she could tell them apart, for they were identical twins. The measure was no longer necessary, for Carmen looked ten years older than Carmela. Simona was there, too, the "mournful widow," as she was know in the village, a nickname that went perfectly with her character. And María, "the martyr," looking twenty years older than her forty-five years, her withered face framed by a black shawl. She was the wife of Don César, and, like everyone else in the village, she knew the double life the "magnate" led. When someone said to her: "Why don't you leave town? Sell a piece of land and go away. You don't have to stand for this," she would shrug her shoulders and answer: "Each night that he sleeps with me is one less sin to his account. If I can take away fifteen or twenty, that will be fifteen or twenty less in the final reckoning." And she would smile the saddest of smiles. Petra, the miller's wife, was the seventh. She was tiny and scrawny, and all the village knew how she had earned the money for the rings and the car she sported, which were the admiration and envy of Torre.

That day they were more nervous than usual, and found the priest's delay almost unbearable. When Don José Antonio finally arrived, they jumped up as though their rear ends had been pricked by a needle. Behind the priest came Pilar, still a girl, though she had been married for seven years. She was Sito's mother, but had had no more children until now, after a long wait, she felt herself in bloom again. Her happiness oozed from every pore, and she bore her swelling bosom with visible pride.

The room in which the circle met was a strange place; its almost triangular form indicated the fact that it had been designed to utilize the angle between the nave and the apse of the church. It held a large table and many chairs. Along the wall ran a border of horrible cheap pictures.

They sat down around the table, and even Don José Antonio, for all his absent-mindedness, was aware of the tension. But the young priest knew that regulations take precedence over problems, and so with complete serenity he ordered the reading of the minutes of the previous meeting, over which Manuela stumbled only six times. Then he began his comments on the Scriptures. His text was St. Luke, Chapter VIII:

And they sailed to the country of the Gerasenes, which is opposite Galilee. Now when he landed, there met him a certain man who for a long time was possessed by a devil, and wore no clothes, and lived in the tombs, not in a house. And when he saw Jesus, he fell down before him, and crying out with a loud voice said, "What have I to do with thee, Jesus, Son of the most high God? I pray thee, do not torment me." For he was charging the unclean spirit to go forth from the man. For many times it had laid hold of him; and he was bound with chains and fetters, and kept under guard, but he would break the bonds asunder, and be driven by the devil into the deserts. And Jesus asked him, saying, "What is thy name?" And he said, "Legion," because many devils had entered into him. And they entreated him not to command them to depart into the abyss.

While Don José Antonio was reading the Scriptures, Elena was thinking: "Doesn't this man realize the kind of world we're living in?"

Simona was thinking: "We know that book of the Gospels by heart."

Petra was thinking: "Always harping on the same thing."

María was thinking: "How that poor man possessed of devils must have suffered."

Carmen was thinking: "What in the devil does this parable matter alongside of what has happened in this village?"

Carmela was thinking: "Alongside of what has happened in this village, what in the devil does this parable matter?"

Manuela was thinking: "The rules say that to expound the Scriptures . . . But, for today . . ."

Don José Antonio went implacably on:

Now a herd of many swine was there, feeding on the mountain-side. And they kept entreating him to

53

give them leave to enter into them. And he gave them leave. And the devils came out from the man and entered into the swine; and the herd rushed down the cliff into the lake and were drowned. And when the swineherds saw what had happened, they fled and reported it in the town and in the country; and people came out to see what had happened. And they came to Jesus, and found the man from whom the devils had gone out sitting at his feet, clothed and in his right mind; and they were afraid. And those also who had seen it reported to them how he had been saved from Legion. And all the people of the Gerasene district besought him to depart from them; for they were seized with great fear.

Don José Antonio closed the book and prepared to expound what he had read. But Manuela could no longer restrain herself.

"Father we are very . . ."

". . . nervous," the twins completed the phrase in unison.

"We would like to know what the Church thinks of these miracles, those of Renato."

The priest of San Martín took a deep breath before answering. "The Church, my daughter, has expressed no opinion as yet, and it is probable that it will be some time before it does so."

"And you, what do you think?" The gray twin talked fast as though she was being chased.

"Yes, what do you think?" The blue one always echoed what her sister said.

"I, my daughters, have no opinion. I was not there. I

only know what you have told me. You who saw it are better judges."

"He doesn't want to go on with the miracles," Simona said. She was thinking of her paralyzed son.

"Charity is the first precept of Christianity, you told us so."

"And now that God has remembered this village . . ."

"That's right. We ought to take advantage of it while it lasts."

"It would be no trouble for Him to send rain."

"Poverty is the cause of many sins."

"Yes, indeed, of many sins," the blue twin asseverated.

They said all this, one interrupting the other, tying the phrases together.

"Yes, it is hard, hard to know what should be done. First of all, we would have to make sure that it was a miracle. And that is very hard to prove. Besides, it would have to be proved that it was the work of God. The devil, too, can work wonders."

"The devil?" Eight voices chorused the words, and six hands leaped to forehead to make the sign of the cross.

"Yes, the devil. Satan is God's monkey, *simia Dei*, don't forget that."

The eight women had the feeling that a strange hand had suddenly put out the light behind the windows.

When through the window Matilde saw Don César coming, she ran to the mirror. She patted her hair, pulled down her sweater, and hurried to the door.

"My love," she greeted him. And as soon as he had closed the door she put her arms around his shoulders. "I thought you weren't coming."

55

"Well, here I am, pet." He kissed her. She ran her hand over the scanty hairs that hid his bald spot.

"Darling, darling." She stretched until her flesh was hard against him, thinking as she did so: "He's getting older every day."

"You're driving me out of my mind."

She snuggled closer, talking in a voice that sounded like a cat in heat: "As soon as summer comes, you forget about me."

"I have to work, sweet."

"I'm jealous of the fields."

"Don't be silly. I have to work. I need money."

"I'm jealous of the money, too."

"If I didn't have it, baby, I couldn't have you."

"Now, that's not true. You know that I love you, just you, not your money." Matilde smiled, a forced smile. She was in low spirits that afternoon. This scene, repeated for the thousandth time, was beginning to bore her. "He's fat," she was thinking, "fatter every day. And dirty." She said: "Why don't you shave, handsome? You'd be so good-looking."

Don César mumbled some excuse, and drew her to him. "You're the one that has to be good-looking. It's enough if you are."

"When will this be over?" she was thinking to herself. She was beginning to feel old herself, and useless. "My last chance," she told herself. "He's over fifty. All this will soon be over for him. And that's the end for me." She made an effort so he would not sense her coldness, for she really found him repulsive. "All my dreams, and to wind up as the mistress of a clodhopper." It was a relief when he let her go.

"I'm tired," he said.

56

"Has anything gone wrong, darling?"

"No. I'm just tired."

"You worry too much. You shouldn't get so involved in things. You come to see me less and less."

It was hard to fawn on a being she hated. She remembered that night ten years before. She had not been able to sleep. "Baby, you're pretty. How would you like to go on the stage?" She had mistrusted the man's looks, but had accepted. She was tired of housework. When she called four days later at the address on the card, she found that the theater was a show wagon that traveled from village to village. When she danced, they told her: "You're no good. But it doesn't matter. Just show plenty of skin." And then: "If you like the profession, here's your contract: board, five hundred pesetas a month, and whatever you can pick up on your own." She was frightened, but she could not turn back. She had proudly told her friends that she was going on the stage. She thought: "I'll try it for a couple of years, and then we'll see. Anyway, it's better than scrubbing floors." But the two years became four, and then Don César appeared on the scene. "Baby, you're beautiful. There's a house waiting for you. I'll set you up in a shop so you won't be bored. How about it?" Matilde had accepted for the sake of a change. She had had a bad time in the village at first, for the young men hung around her house, and the women swore they would not set foot inside her shop. But time had worn down the rough edges. The young men, without having given up making a play for her, bothered her less, and little by little the women had forgotten their vow. Now, six years later, there were very few who remained faithful to their "I'd rather starve than buy from a heretic," and Matilde's status had, in a way, become legalized, for people accepted the situation as normal. Don César had substituted his visits to Matilde's house for his trips to Irola. What was the difference? people said.

But now she was beginning to feel depressed. It bored her to spend the day weighing out paprika and wrapping up bars of chocolate. But the hours she had to endure Don César were even more boring. She hated to have to make the effort to excite him, to make herself necessary to him so that when he left he would leave a bill on the table.

"What's worrying you now, dear?"

"It doesn't rain."

"What do you care? You're not going to go hungry."

"I need another threshing machine," he answered. "There would still be a good harvest if it would rain. If it doesn't, it's going to be a calamity. I stand to lose more than the whole village put together."

"You're right, dear." It did not seem good strategy to contradict him. She would have loved to say: "You'll eat without another threshing machine. But the villagers are going to starve." What she said was: "Don't worry, love. Haven't you got me? Come on, love me."

And she raised her parted lips. At that moment the church bell began the Angelus. And Matilde felt a vague longing to be in the church. As Don César had not noticed her raised lips, she lowered her head.

In Irola, too, the matter was being commented on.

The mayor's wife had said to him: "You know what they told the maid at market? That in some village, I don't know just where, a cross had fallen into a lake and a man brought it up just by praying from the bank."

The mayor laughed so hard that some of his soup splashed on his wife's dress all the way across the table.

The Bishop had said: "Why don't they give the Virgin a rest?" Because, according to his secretary, the Virgin had appeared to a train switchman. He did not know exactly where it had happened. Some said in San Martín, others in Torre.

In Torre the noon bell was ringing. Renato asked himself what he needed to be happy. "This is over. It will take them a while to forget it, but it will be forgotten." He had just sent the twelve-o'clock freight through, and had felt as he did so that now everything was back to normal, as though the freight train had carried off the miracle with the rest of its merchandise.

The memory was still fresh, but that morning he had been almost happy after the sufferings of the day before. It had annoyed him to feel all eyes on him at Mass, but now he felt free, and even thought that the village had understood him.

It was a beautiful morning. There was a real spring sun, and the grove in which the Los Setos road ended a few yards from his house was humming with new life. From the village came the echo of the dance music of feast-day noons.

"Everything is back to normal," he said. And, raising his head to the sky, he smiled. "Don't play any more of these jokes."

5 But Renato was wrong. That had been only a truce, and a very short one, broken the next day by the presence of Lucio and Don José Antonio. And afterward by Manuela, by Doña Asunción, and by Simona.

It was thus that the siege began, the encirclement that grew tighter with every passing day.

"But what is it you want of me?" he asked.

Don José Antonio had said to him: "Explain it to me."

"I have nothing to explain, Father."

And so it was. He had nothing to explain. Renato had asked himself why those things had happened, and he could find nothing that would help.

"What did you feel?"

"I don't know. Empty, maybe."

"Empty?"

"Yes, hollow, as though I had no flesh. But . . ."

"But?"

"At the same time, maybe, fuller than ever. But full of the other."

"Of the other? Which other?"

"How do I know?"

"And then what?"

"Then tired. As though I had been loading sacks all day."

And these same answers, over and over. And locking the door. And opening it in desperation at the knocks. And getting out of bed at night.

"Everything, I'd give you everything."

And shaking his head. And shutting the door. And hearing the weeping on the other side.

Then one day a car stopped at his door.

"I have brought you my daughter. She has cancer. Nobody can cure her. I have taken her to Switzerland, and they can't help her. We are good Christians. We have gone to Lourdes, to Fatima. Cure her, for God's sake. She's all I have."

"You're mistaken. This village is not Lourdes."

"You won't regret it if you cure her."

"I'm telling you again, this is not Lourdes."

"At least pray for her recovery."

"I'll pray, but it is useless. I have no key to miracles. That is in the hand of God and only God."

Renato turned to the girl. Her lusterless eyes were fixed on him in supplication. He said to her: "Health is not the most important thing in the world. Your soul is not sick, and that is what matters."

"But I cannot enjoy her soul," her father shouted. "I need her life; she is my only child, and we are alone. My wife . . . left us a year ago. I am rich, I can . . ."

"Be quiet. Don't blaspheme."

The man got furiously into the car. Renato had said to him: "An only child? Why?"

Without answering, the man drove off, the girl stretched out on the back seat. All Renato could remember now were those pure eyes. He remembered, too, that as he looked into them he had been afraid, for a strange trembling had shaken his body as on the occasions of the cross and the canary.

From time to time, between trains, Renato went out to walk in the fields. He saw the pallid, parched wheat that was not heading, and it gave him the feeling that he was to blame. At moments he felt a strange happiness: "Only suffering saves." He recalled this phrase, heard he could not remember where, and it occurred to him that Torre was being purified.

It had been a year without spring, and by May it was already summer. The sky was vast, and rarely did the fleece of a cloud cross the firmament. The quiet continued unbroken.

His night walks grew more frequent. Having to get up to send the quarter-of-five train through brought him wide awake, and it was hard for him to go back to sleep. Then he would leave his house before even the earliest farmer was up, and cross the village under the silence of the moon. It seemed to him that he could hear the heartbeats of all the inhabitants. An occasional light revealed the sources of babies' cries. At such moments Renato felt closer to all of them, and he thought that he would give his life to help them. "All, I would give all, if God asked it of me." With the stir of the morning breeze it seemed to him that his soul was freshly watered and that he was at peace with God and the world. It was as though his soul were buoyed up, like the body when in water. Then he felt a desire to pray and said the Lord's Prayer over and over very softly. He repeated it without realizing what he was saying; the words were mere sounds or cabalistic signs, but that was all he needed to feel near to God. It seemed to him that from one of the houses came the distant song of children at play:

62

> *I have a dolly*
> *Dressed in blue*

But the village was sleeping and silence hung over every door. And yet:

> *With a white veil*
> *And a guimpe, too.*

The stars, too, were silent in the sky. Then:

> *I took her walking*
> *She caught a cold*

Perhaps he was hearing the angels—or God Himself—singing:

> *I've put her to bed*
> *And she's very sick.*

He buried his hands in his pockets and went home whistling. Then he took out his colored balls and began to juggle them, faster and faster. He remembered the performances in the theaters improvised in the squares of the villages, and heard again the spectators' laughter. There came back to his memory—with every detail—the scene of the two strangled women, and the photograph of the man, riddled with bullets, which had appeared in the newspapers. And he said: "You know that he was good, Lord. He made the people laugh. That was good, Lord. The kindest act of charity." And he tossed the balls faster and faster as though he was in front of a gaping audience. He seemed to hear: "And now, friends, ladies and gentlemen, get ready to give Chico a big hand, the child wonder of the age, the fastest juggler on the face of the earth." And then came the applause. "You've got a great future ahead of you, Chico. After the balls, you will learn to handle the plates and then the knives. You will be a star, kid." But Renato had not gone on. When the tragedy had occurred, he had only known how to handle the balls, and he went no further. Six colored balls were his only souvenir of childhood. And that was enough.

These were the moments when Renato was happy. But as soon as it struck six he could see in his mind's eye all the farmers of the village getting up and looking at the sky. He could hear: "You're not going back to bed?"

"What the hell are we going to do in the fields?" And then the wife's smothered weeping.

And the same thing repeated six, ten, forty times, in each farmhouse of the village. And at each oath he dropped a ball.

So it went, one day and another. The moon changed once, twice, and everything went on the same, as though time were nailed down.

"It rained today in San Martín," came the word one day. And four days later: "It rained all afternoon in Grijalba."

In the tavern Uncle Lucas's pipe went out. The radio had just given the noon news report: "There is promise of a good harvest in all the provinces of Castile. Grains . . ."

"Turn off that radio," Martín shouted. El Moro obeyed. A silence followed. "This is a punishment," Uncle Lucas said.

The month of May went by. And June. Two days before St. John's feast, the women said: "By this time the reaping had always begun."

"And . . . what are we going to reap this year?"

St. John's Day was a sad day that seemed as if it would never end. The town-hall clock might have been brand-new, for it seemed to all that it struck the hours louder than ever before.

In the tavern Lucio said: "There's only one thing to do."

Several pairs of eyes turned toward him. "Renato?" Uncle Lucas asked. "Yes. He's preventing it." Lucio observed that the eyes became hard. He went on: "It's all his fault that it does not rain. We'll have to . . . eliminate him."

Now the eyes turned toward Uncle Lucas. He lowered his head. "That would only make things worse. That would be the end. Yes, the end." And then: "There's only one solution." He set his teeth. "For us all to die of hunger."

The silence that followed was prolonged.

"Why, why does he refuse?" Martín asked.

Doña Julia said it was to make himself the center of attention. "That's what he wants, for us to beg him. It's nothing more than that. As though I didn't know. To have the whole village running after him, to know that he is the topic of conversation in every house."

Doña Julia laughed as she said this. Hers was a superior laugh, different from all the others in the village. She patted her complicated coiffure, smoothed down the back of her skirt, and drew her figure up even straighter.

"If only your father were alive . . . He was the only one who knew how to handle such matters. These priests —what can you expect of them? The one is an old man and the other isn't dry behind the ears yet. And both of them without the slightest culture." (She pronounced the word as though it were written with a *K*). "Now, your father . . ."

She ran her eyes over Telesforo's library, the pride of her heart, carefully shelved in the sitting-room to impress "all these bumpkins who come to see me." She caressed the backs of the books with her eyes and drifted off on a sea of memories.

Across from her, Magdalena sat as though far away. She was very pale and her appearance was that of a child, too much so for her eighteen years. She looked odd with her braids and white-collared pinafore. The meal ended without the girl's saying a single word. Only when it was over did she speak: "I'm going to lie down."

"Don't you feel well?"

"I'm tired, that's all."

"It's because you don't eat. Your face is like a knife, and you're as pale as . . ."

"That's just your imagination, Mama."

When she got to her room, Magdalena sat down in a rocker and drew a deep breath. She felt dizzy and nauseated. After she had thrown up she felt better. She stood before the mirror and unbraided her hair. She shook her head, and her hair spread from shoulder to shoulder like a shower of honey. She felt freer without the braids, less of a child. Her hair was so pretty, like old gold.

She heard the house door close, and ran to the window to make sure mother had gone out. She was both happy and enraged as she saw her going into the house across the way, to Don Ricardo's *tertulia*. Her heels clicked lightly on the stairs as she went down, unbuttoning her dress on the way. In her mother's room she threw her pinafore on the floor and took one of her mother's four dresses off the hanger. After she had put on the green one, she looked

66

at herself in the mirror. "I'm almost a woman. I'm as tall as she is."

She gave a half-turn and smoothed back her hair. She picked up her frock from the floor, and her eyes welled over with tears. "I'm not a child any more. I'm eighteen years old. Eighteen. Why do I always have to dress like a kid?"

Magdalena did not, could not understand it. She did not know that by dressing her as a child Doña Julia consoled herself for the passing of the years. Because she wanted to feel young, had to feel young, and to accept the fact that she had a grown daughter would have shattered this illusion. How could she go on thinking that she was still in her salad years if she was confronted four times a day with a daughter whose flesh flaunted her youth? She had to prolong those braids, those dresses. "Why, baby, you are still just a little girl. It was only yesterday that I held you in my arms." Yes, Doña Julia had to believe she was still young, or, at any rate, give that appearance. Otherwise how could she keep Don Ricardo at her heels?

"I wish Rodrigo could see me like this." A flood of tenderness filled Magdalena as she thought of him. "I'd give anything." And then: "Why do I love him so much?"

Magdalena could not understand this either, just as she could not understand the trembling that had seized her when they had been together the first time, and then the first day he had kissed her, and that day in the old convent.

"The convent, it's all the fault of the convent that the young ones start running before they can walk," was the dictum of the village. This was because the ruined convent was the meeting-place for lovers.

But in this case the convent was not wholly to blame; it was the dresses, the braids, the old furniture that smothered Magdalena.

"When I'm with you it is as though I were beginning another life."

And it was another life that had begun. It was a life of love that had succeeded that of hypocrisy, ignorance, farce. The first days had brought complete happiness, a joy such as Magdalena had never dreamed could exist. Then there had come a change, and the life of passion had begun, a life almost of hatred, with its oscillation between delight and depression.

Magdalena had closed her eyes and had given herself over to the unknown, for even though she sensed that this was not right, it seemed to her better than what had gone on before. But, even so, at times she longed for the happiness of the first days.

"Now my mother is . . ." she thought. And she clenched her fists until they hurt.

Rodrigo had said to her one day: "Your mother will understand. She and Don Ricardo are intimate too."

Magdalena felt as though she had been touched by a live wire. "What did you say?"

She was trembling, and he put his arms around her. "The whole town knows it, my girl."

Magdalena was stunned. Then suddenly she felt in her heart a fierce hatred for her mother. If Doña Julia had been there at that moment, she would have felt the courage to strike her. Rodrigo was drawing her to him, and for the first time she put up no resistance. A smile began in her eyes, a bitter smile that did not go with her expression. But she let it grow. She had hit upon her revenge. And when her eyes clouded, she did not think of God; her one thought was that this would make her mother suffer, and that thought filled her with happiness. Although this was quickly followed by sadness, it was still mixed with happiness.

She looked at herself in the mirror. She recalled their conversation the day before: "I'm afraid. She's going to notice it any day. It's getting very noticeable."

"Put on a loose dress," he had answered.

"That won't help. It's very noticeable. Besides, I'm throwing up a lot. It's a good thing she's not at home much."

He hugged her. "I hope it's a boy."

She laughed, and then became very serious. "What do you think she will say when she finds out?"

He did not dare answer her question. "It would be better if we were married when it comes."

"What if she won't let us?"

"She has to," he said excitedly, "she has to."

Magdalena began to cry. "She won't let us. I know she won't."

Midsummer Night was a sad night. More out of habit than for any other reason, the village lads gathered to garland the windows. It was a clear night, and the footsteps lacked all air of mystery. The dry wood was already piled in the square and the bonfire was lighted.

It was then that Uncle Lucas, Julián, and Martín left the tavern. They stopped, watching the bonfire from a distance.

"Hey, Martín, you not going to the bonfire? Or are you too old?"

Martín moved forward. The flames projected the

shadow of his heavy body against the church. The shadow moved with a lurching gait. "You idiots," he said. "You still feel like playing the fool?"

The bonfire was crackling, and the flames were higher than a man's head. The circle of lads opened. And he moved closer.

"What are you going to do?"

Bending over, he picked up a stave that had not yet caught fire, and looked at his companions as though giving himself time. Then he raised the stave and the lads fell back several paces. The bonfire was crackling like a falling house, and the flames spurted in all directions.

"You're going to get burned." But Martín went on beating the bonfire until the glowing embers were scattered all over the square.

"Anyone who laughs tonight is going to find a knife between his ribs," he said.

The square resembled a starry sky. But at four in the morning, when Nicolás crossed it on the run, not one live coal remained. The Paseo de Los Setos seemed to him longer than ever. He pounded on Renato's door, shouting: "She's dying on me."

The switchman rubbed his eyes.

"It's Pilar, she's dying."

Renato answered: "I have to send the train through."

And Nicolás: "She's dying."

Renato: "No, not yet."

Then he asked himself why he had said that. He went on: "I'll go as soon as the train comes through."

"Will you cure her?"

"I'll go."

"God help us."

Renato watched Nicolás walk away. Slowly at first, then faster, until he disappeared among the trees. It was quarter past four. Renato sat down on the bench by the door. He wanted to think, but his head felt hollow, and he could not concentrate on anything. He had lost all notion of time, sitting there with his head buried in his hands, and it was only when the train whistled at the station that he went over to the switches and moved them slowly, as though performing a sacramental rite. The train went chugging past. Behind the windows the sleeping people were huddled.

He set out for the town, and saw the fields to left and to right with their withered, drooping stalks. "They are not cutting them," he said to himself.

Dawn was breaking, and little by little Renato came back to reality. His head was filling up.

Pilar lay in bed drenched in sweat. She had braided her hair in a single braid so it would bother her less, and it was soaked in perspiration. From the rumpled sheets her arms emerged, and the nails of her hands were buried in the rails of the headboard. "At last," said Maneras. And he stood there waiting for Renato to do something.

The switchman went over to the bed. "Does it hurt?"

"As though I were being broken in two." It was a thread of a voice. She was painfully thin, and she was panting. Renato looked at Don Melquíades, whose head was bowed. The room smelled badly. They went out.

"There's nothing to do. She's very weak. She won't be able to hold out. Please God we can save the child."

"There's nothing to do?" Renato asked.

"Afloverin," said the doctor. "Perhaps afloverin." And then: "But it's expensive." And to Nicolás: "You ought to go for it." He took a deep breath. "Well, I'm going. This is going slowly. Perhaps nothing will happen till tomorrow. Call me if there's any change."

"Good-by, Doctor." Nicolás bowed.

They went into the room. She asked: "What did he say?"

"That it's going slow. Not till tomorrow."

There was a long silence broken only by the woman's breathing. Renato felt Nicolás's eyes on him painfully. To break the silence, he said: "The . . . what the doctor said . . . maybe . . . ?"

"And where am I to get the money? I've been out of work since December. Thanks to the kid, we've made out. He gets seven pesetas for tending the sheep. It's not much. I've had to pawn everything." After a pause he added: "I was counting on the harvest."

"There's money in the village."

"In the village . . ." Maneras's jaw tightened as he said the words.

Renato raised his head. "How much? How much is needed?"

"Nearly three thousand."

Renato started for the door. "You wait for me."

"Where are you going?"

Renato was smiling now. "I have seven hundred. I'll find the rest. You wait and see."

Maneras shook his head. "It's useless. You're just wasting your time."

"You wait." And Renato left.

The switchman, on the way back from his house with the seven hundred pesetas in his pocket, realized that for the first time he had not been asked for a miracle. "We'll fix this up without a miracle," he thought to himself.

But in this Renato was deluded. Uncle Lucas said: "With the year we are facing, everything is going to be too little. Two thousand pesetas? Nothing small about you!"

Don César received him in the cow barn. Ten fine animals were feeding along the double row of mangers.

"See here, why don't you put your mind to working a miracle instead of going from house to house begging? It would come out much cheaper. You can say a rosary in ten minutes, can't you?" He laughed as he said this. Then he went on harshly: "If you think the people here are going to help you, you're mad. Or don't you think you've made us lose enough?"

María Belén stood listening and twisting a button of her smock. When Renato left, the girl followed him, limping on her short leg. She dragged the foot in the thick-soled shoe. "Renato," she said to him, "my mother says she wants to talk to you. You're to come to the back door."

The switchman smiled. He walked slowly so as not to hurry the girl's pace. She went on: "I would like to help you." He laid his hand on her head. "But all my dolls are broken." Renato stroked her braids. The girl looked at him.

"You could . . ." She hesitated.

"I could what?"

". . . sell the canary. It cost eighty pesetas."

María was waiting for him at the back door. "This is all I've got," she said. "These earrings. He gave them to me when we were engaged. I think they are worth a lot. Over three thousand."

Renato could say only: "Thanks."

"For what?" She smiled.

73

Now Renato was happy. He thought to himself: "If it isn't enough, I'll sell my bed." But he had to hurry to get to the capital and sell the earrings and buy the medicine. The clock was striking ten as Renato crossed the plaza toward Maneras's house. He was smiling.

At that moment he saw Sito running toward him.

"My father says . . ." He burst into tears. The box holding the earrings broke in Renato's hand. The bells began to toll.

Down the street flickered the tapers escorting the cross. Lucio's voice, high-pitched like a rabbit's, was muttering prayers in Latin. He was dressed in black, and his armless left sleeve hung limp, black and white. In his right hand he carried a book stained with blots. *Miserere mei Deus secundum magnam misericordiam tuam.* Behind him four village lads carried on their shoulders the body of Pilar, beside which the bluish flesh of her new-born child nestled. A cruel sun beat straight down, and the street was covered with powdery dust that filled the throat. *Et secundum multitudinem miserationum tuarum dele iniquitatem meam.* The whole village was following the coffin. Some of the women were weeping. The men were talking, some of them even laughing surreptitiously. Nicolás's eyes were red. Sito looked at everything as though seeing it for the first time. *Amplius lava me ab iniquitate mea et a peccato meo munda me.* When they passed by the cross, all the men clenched their teeth. Blasphemy was in all hearts and on some lips. *Nam iniquitatem meam ego cognosco et peccatum meum contra me est semper.* The grainless stalks of wheat swayed in the wind. The threshing-floors lay bare. *Tibi soli peccavi et malum coram te feci.* There was hate in each and every

74

heart. All the curses were on Renato. "He did not come," they said. "There's a reason for it." *Ecce enim in iniquitatibus conceptus sum et in peccatis concepit me mater mea.* "He's a switchman. What does he care whether it rains or not?" Ahead of the tapers went the colorful rows of children, running, jumping, as on a vacation morning. *Fac me audire gaudium et lætitiam et exultabunt ossa humiliata.* "Why didn't he prevent this death? Why didn't he work a miracle?" This was Don César's question. The rows of children stretched farther, and the reds and blues glowed amid the dust and the sun. *Redde mihi lætitiam salutaris tui et spiritu principali confirma me.* Maneras recalled how Renato had come into the dead woman's room. "Forgive me," he had said. The tapers and the cross reached the cemetery, and the tin door squeaked lazily. *Domine, labia mea aperies et os meum anuntiabit laudem tuam.* When Pilar had begun to die, she had said: "Tell Renato I understand, and I thank him." Renato had left the money and the earrings on the table. "For Masses," he said. *Sacrificium Deo spiritus contribulatus, cor contritum et humiliatum Deus non despicies.* "Hate has entered this village. I don't know how, but it has entered," Don José Antonio was thinking. *Benigne fac Domine in bona voluntate tua Sion ut edificentur muri Jerusalem.* Between two ropes the coffin descended slowly. The first clods of earth fell with dull thuds that set many to trembling. *Tunc acceptabis sacrificia, oblationes et holocausta, tunc imponent super altare tuum vitulos.* "Peace, peace to the dead," Don José Antonio murmured. The town-hall clock struck twelve. "And peace to the living, too," he added.

75

6

Don José Antonio was pacing the floor nervously.

Don Macario said: "Yes, my son. We are living on God's very frontier, and a frontier is never a comfortable spot. To be sure, you can smuggle things through occasionally; there is better tobacco, better coffee. But think of the drawbacks. Always under police surveillance, knowing that in the event of war your town will be the first to fall. That's the state of our village. There are certain advantages: an occasional bootlegged miracle, but when war breaks out . . . And it has already broken out here."

Don Macario stirred in his bed. "I have come to the conclusion," he went on, "that God is constantly changing frontiers. He comes down, sets up his tents beside one city, and then another, and another, and another. There may even be a moment when God is on the frontier of each soul, that decisive moment in life when a person knows that everything is at stake. It is that moment of absolute aloneness when a man stands naked before God, without one human handhold. When that moment comes to the soul, there are few paths to choose from. Before, when I was young, I thought there were only two: either to give oneself up to God or to kill Him; I mean kill the idea of Him, the one we men hold. Later I saw that there was another: to become indifferent and go on living. If this moment has not yet come to you, I may tell you that this third path is the worst, but it is also the most comfortable . . . and the most frequented."

The sound of the priest's labored breathing was as audible as the ticking of a clock. It was hard to say whether his smile was gay or sad, so intermingled were joy and sorrow in it. He went on: "You know that my reading now is limited to the Bible and my breviary. Now, something that has always interested me is the reason for the death of the prophets. Nearly all of them were put to death, like Christ. And it is always the same. It was God who drew up his frontier in Israel, who sank his spurs into the flanks of the Chosen People, who rode them. And there was always someone who gave himself to Him and ended up murdered. The same thing happened with the saints. All the true saints have died crucified—in one way or another, but crucified. Perhaps blood is the only thing that redeems."

Don Macario became silent. The tick-tock of his breathing could be clearly heard.

Don José Antonio said: "God's frontier . . . What if it were really the devil's frontier?"

"Could be. Perhaps it is the devil's frontier too. Not only possible, but very probable. Maybe we are bounded by God on the east and the devil on the west. The devil always walks in God's footsteps. If it did not sound like heresy, I'd say he was His shadow. Ah, the lukewarm are already his. They will not go either backward or forward. They may be free of all sins except one—that of doing nothing, and that is enough for Satan to send them to his kingdom. But he is far more concerned about real sinners and saints, far more."

"But everything was going well here. Everyone at-

77

tended Mass on Sunday, made confession during Holy Week, and received the sacraments. There was a visible improvement. But now everything is saturated with hate."

"Everything was going well . . . everything was going well. No, son. I don't know if there was hate before or not. But I can assure you that love did not exist. Do you remember the '*etiam peccata*' of St. Augustine? Also the sins, also. Toward love there is one straight road: love. All the others are devious. But of them the shortest is hate, which so often is only a way of love, a disguise."

"But this is worse. You can see it, touch it."

"True, it can be seen, touched more than before. But it was the same. The lake was still, but in its depths were the lures, the decay. Whereas now . . ."

"You are defending . . ."

"I am not defending anybody. I am not up to any kind of defense any more. Don Melquíades is amazed at how this old patched-up rattletrap still holds together. The most I can defend now is six feet of ground under the cypresses. And hope that God will have mercy on my stupidity."

There was a long silence. Don Macario coughed a number of times. "They say that lucidity comes at the hour of death. Maybe it is that at the hour of lucidity death comes. Yes, I believe that understanding everything is more than enough reason for us to die. If we could understand God as He is, if we could suddenly see how ridiculous our lives are, we could not go on living. Listen to me: a great many of the saints died young, and all of them, all of them have had a bad time in this life. One cannot serve two masters. Ah, and such joys as they know are foretastes of heaven. It is a different kind of happiness, a happiness that none of us, the mediocre, could resist."

"But God, isn't He a consolation?"

"Son, God is love, then truth, then, long after that, consolation. Long after that. And yet, yet . . ." He did not venture to say what he was thinking. It seemed to him hypocrisy to talk of sanctity.

"Son, in the light of death one sees many things. As, for example, that one has been a coward. I have only one consolation: knowing that I have been honest with my cowardice, that I have not lied to myself. Others are cowards and they cover it up with plans and works. And they are cowards, nothing but cowards. They work, they come and go, they preach, they organize, and it is all cowardice. The priesthood is a very hard thing—now I understand it. It is not doing this or doing that, but doing everything with a different tone."

"The saints were active."

"Not always. There you have Christ: he spent thirty years pounding nails and sawing pieces of wood that have not even come down to us as relics, and only three years preaching. And don't try to tell me that he was preparing himself in those years, because I can't imagine what in the devil God had to prepare Himself for. When you have Him within you, it makes no difference whether you peel potatoes or pray. And if God is lacking, nothing a man does is of more consequence than the acts of a mouse. For that reason I am afraid for you young people. You think yourselves better because you work. But you are just as bourgeois with your card catalogues as we with our games of cards. That's not what counts, my friend. God's frontier . . . Yes, it is shameful that He has to come down to our side of the street."

79

The two priests were silent for a long time. Don Macario had sunk back on his pillows, and Don José Antonio was pacing nervously back and forth. Finally he said: "The thought of next winter frightens me."

"Yes, me too. But I am much more afraid of happiness. When everything is going well, man comes to think there is no God or to live as though he thought so."

"They will curse God."

"So they will, but I don't know which is worse, blasphemy or heedlessness. The one who blasphemes at least feels himself bound, tied to someone, dependent. Even though perhaps it were better that nothing of this sort had happened. Better for men, I mean. It is always to be hoped that God will take pity on our emptiness. But it must be very discouraging for God to save men only because they have no sins in their knapsack. Can the one who struggles to fill his with wheat be sure he has put in no stones? The one who feels sure that he is carrying no tares is the one whose soul is completely empty."

Don Macario stirred in his bed, and smiled. "But I am boring you with sermons. Forgive me. These long days alone fill the head with questions. Yes, that is the worst of solitude, that one finds the answer and lacks the courage to live it. Fortunately, I am going to live a very short time, but now, after what I have seen, it would be so hard for me to begin. What a lucky thing it is to die. I am afraid of being a saint."

"It is beautiful to be a saint."

"Yes, it is beautiful. Just as the crucifixion is beautiful."

And the tide of hunger rolled over the village, a raging tide that left no corner untouched. It entered the houses, striking first the children, the aged, and then finally the fathers and the mothers. Out of boxes came the last of the savings; the quarreling over bones in the butcher shop, and the selling of blankets and mattresses. And the coat bought the year before when the crop had been good. And the dower coins, and the wedding dress.

"And for this?"

"A hundred pesetas."

"It cost us six hundred."

"A hundred pesetas."

"But it's new, brand-new. It's only been worn three times."

"A hundred pesetas."

And the garment became another's property.

"No, Juan, not that. No."

"But, woman, we have no choice."

"It's the only thing I've got to remember Mother by."

"We need food. You can't eat fans."

"Get a good price. It's ivory."

"Only eighty pesetas?"

"And that's more than it's worth. It will all have to be made over."

"It's ivory."

"It's broken."

"No, Mariano, not the mattress. What will we do when winter comes? The children will freeze to death."

"And now they are going to starve to death."

"Two hundred pesetas for a mattress like this?"

"Two hundred pesetas."

.   .   .

And the stealing began. Orchards, bakeries, and granaries were under constant threat. Everything had suddenly become a problem.

Don César shouted: "I'm going to spend the night in the barn lot with a loaded shotgun. And anyone that shows up will get it."

And Uncle Lucas: "I know you have sold the wagon and the mule. It's about time you paid me back the fifteen hundred pesetas I lent you in January."

There is no waiting. The courts do not wait.

"And how long can this go on?"

"If it would only rain, there would still be grapes."

"And if it doesn't, there'll be no work until planting."

"That is, if anyone decides to plant."

"They say they are not going to plant any more, that the land is cursed."

"Yes, cursed. The land."

It was then that the letter came. "They have opened a new shaft in the mine and need people. If you come right away . . ."

And they must go, go quickly, leaving wives and children. Quickly, quickly. Miles and miles by train.

"Twenty-seven? We only need six."

And there, where are they to live? They'll have to build a house of sheets of tin. And the letters: "We are well. We'll soon be sending you money." And the women's letters: "Save all you can. It will still not be enough." And the men: "I am enclosing two hundred. At first there are a lot of expenses."

And the hours spent in the tavern to forget their loneliness at any cost.

And the women: "What do they do there by themselves?"

"Mine doesn't send much. He's probably spending it on . . ."

These were the six lucky ones. The rest pushed on, and after a month of fruitless looking for work, the last eleven came back gaunt and sad.

"If we have to die, it's better among our own."

The tide of hunger rose.

"Juana's boy is sick."

"Yes, it's his lungs."

"This child needs fresh air. And to sleep by himself."

"Where, Doctor?"

"He's going to give it to the others. Please God we don't get an epidemic in the village now. That's all we need."

And Renato's name on every lip. And he: "Lord, do You think we deserved this? I can't ask You to work miracles . . . But do something about this."

And the voice of his angel: "There's money in the village. If the rich would open up their granaries, there would be enough."

"But don't make the innocent pay for the guilty. . . ."

The angel went on: "And the poor . . . how much did they spend on celebrations last year?"

"How did they know? They had just received their summer's pay, and they never expected this."

"And what about the money squandered in the tavern?"

"They have to. It's the only place they can dream."

"The only place?"

"Yes, the only place. The houses are dirty, the women

unkempt, the children in rags. In the tavern at least they can forget that they are living. The only other place is the church. And the church . . ."

"What about the church?"

"It is too beautiful a dream for them."

And the woman came shivering with fever. "My Juanito is dying."

"Take this."

And a cry: "No, I did not come to beg alms. Better all of us dead than that."

"Then why did you come?"

"I don't know. I just came."

The business of the "bread of the poor" happened about this time. Everyone remembered the appearance of the car in the square. Someone had said: "It's the bread of the poor." And the name had stuck.

For everybody knew that the miller had become rich on the black market.

"If you want me to do your grinding, you'll have to give me one sack for every three."

The grinding had to be done at any price, but the bitterness corroded the soul. "The millers," that strangely dwarfish and anemic couple, suddenly felt themselves important. They played a major role in the life of the village, and their bank account began to rise like the mercury in a thermometer when you put a match to it. The miller's wife laughed. "Paco, I want you to buy me a car; I want everybody to see how rich we are. Do you remember the big one the Condes had? I want one like that."

"But that costs a fortune. . . ."

"We've got it, haven't we?"

Paco had always been a poor devil, and she was the one

who ran the business. But Petra liked to pretend her husband had the power to deny or concede her what she asked for.

And so one afternoon the two of them went to the capital and came back with a car out of a fairy tale. Paco was thinking on the way home: "This was crazy. We should have bought something plain." But his wife had made up her mind to buy the best there was in Madrid, and it had eaten a big hole in their profits.

All this was running through Paco's mind while Arturo, the young chauffeur, fitted out in a fine new suit, was fulfilling the first part of his contract. At that moment Paco, to his great surprise, felt Petra's arm around his shoulder.

"My dear, you are a prince." Her eyes were gleaming. "I am happy, really happy."

A ripple of desire ran through Paco and he felt like kissing her. But he controlled himself. He recalled their marriage long before, he the son of a baker, she the miller's daughter.

"No, I don't want any children," she had said. And he had kept quiet because he had never dared to contradict her.

But today he felt a new warmth about her, something that he could not recall in all their thirty years of marriage. Hesitatingly he put his arm around her waist. He tried to kiss her, but she avoided him.

"Don't be silly." She had laughed softly, with a gesture toward the chauffeur. And as she looked at him in the mirror, Petra realized that Arturo was not bad looking.

When the car glided to a stop in the square, Petra's cup of happiness brimmed over. Curtains stirred behind the windowpanes. The squeals of the children brought the people from the side streets. Petra would have liked it if people had come up to the car, but the men eyed it from a distance as though it bore a contagion. Only the children touched the tires and windows one by one. She felt like a heroine as she stepped out, with Arturo holding the door, and she rewarded him with a wide, prolonged smile. As she proceeded toward her house, she asked herself which she was prouder of, the magnificent car or her young, elegant chauffeur.

The next morning the whole village was shocked to learn that when Petra had called the miller, she had found him dead. The phrase "a judgment of God" was on everyone's lips. She suffered more from the shock of his unexpected death than because of her affection for him. She repeated a thousand times: "He was a saint," and even managed to squeeze out a dozen tears.

But it was then that her torment began. The village noticed how she frequented the confessional, and they all thought her husband's death had affected her deeply and that she was going to return their ill-gotten gains. But that was not what Petra talked about as she knelt before Don José Antonio.

"Father, I accuse myself of desire, of thought and wish, a hundred thousand times a day."

"Does he know it?"

"No, he knows nothing."

"My daughter, avoid every occasion."

"Father, that is not possible. He lives in the house. I see him every minute, and every minute I am filled with impure thoughts and desires. I would give my very life to be his."

"Daughter, that is a sin."

"I would go to hell if I knew that there I could embrace him."

And so day after day. Meanwhile, Arturo spent the idle hours stretched out in one chair with his feet on another, devouring veritable mountains of cheap novels. It filled him with pride to know that he was the focus of attention in the village. (In the bakery a sudden need for more bread on the part of the girls became evident.) But he liked to play hard to get, a role that he had learned from American movies, and he fell in love with the part.

He felt real repugnance for the miller's widow. He watched her come and go, overwhelming him with cosseting, with attentions, sitting alongside him in silence for hours. It amused him to see her suffer, to turn a deaf ear to her insinuations, which grew bolder and bolder as time went on. These tactics were successful, for by blowing hot and cold he became the absolute master, not only of the house's one inhabitant, but of everything else in the house.

But one day Arturo got fed up with this amusement, and he thought of another game that would be quicker and surer. This was to make off with the car and everything in the house worth taking. When Petra found him gone, she burst into tears. But her tears lasted only two hours, for by that time she had found out that the bird had not flown the coop with empty claws.

The car was found abandoned near the station of Medina del Campo, but neither hide nor hair of Arturo was ever seen again. The chauffeur who brought the car back to Torre was an old man of seventy who left by train the next day, and the car sat in solitary splendor in the carriage shed. Only in the morning, in the early hours, did it receive the daily visit of its owner, who dusted it carefully to have it in proper shape when Arturo returned.

It was around January when he had cleared out, and the following months had been a time of great suffering for Petra. Economically, too. She had had to learn to hold off payments, for the mill stood completely idle. One day she realized that the most useless possession she owned was the car. She resisted the temptation for two months. But one day it became clear to her that Arturo was not coming back, and that the only way to efface his memory was to get rid of the last link that bound her to him.

She wrote out the following advertisement: *For sale: Buick, latest model, like new, in perfect condition. Torre de Muza, Plaza José Antonio.*

And when she read the advertisement in the newspaper, she realized that she burned her bridges behind her.

Those two men knew cars. They drove the "bread of the poor" out of the carriage shed, and in the middle of the square raised the hood and gave the motor a careful going-over. This gave the whole village time to learn what had happened, and all drew near the square with open or covert curiosity.

Then the one wearing glasses got behind the wheel while the fat one with the cigar laughed at the workout he gave it. He drove it in first, in second, in third, in reverse, and then in first again; he made two turns around the fountain, and then circled the fountain again, this time in reverse.

While the men were going through all these operations, the miller's widow felt as though every change of gear was squeezing her heart.

The men paid her, and when the car drove out of the square and disappeared in the dust of the road, the whole village felt as though something living had been torn out of it by the roots. And they realized that, at heart, they had not hated the "bread of the poor" and had even felt proud of having in their village the best car in the whole vicinity. And that its loss was a real come-down for Torre. Once more Renato was held responsible for everything with his drought.

◇◇◇◇◇◇◇◇◇◇◇

7 "Always reading the Old Testament," Don José Antonio remarked. "Why that preference?"

Don Macario laughed. "Son, it's to make up for people's neglect of it. Even the priests. For the majority, the Word of God is limited to the four Gospels. Some get as far as the Epistles, but not beyond them. The God of the prophets seems to them a God of the reserves, a second-division God, as you young folks would say."

"But the God of the New Testament is the God of love, the Christian God."

Don Macario eyed him with an ironic smile. "Christian God! That's a good one. As though God the Creator weren't."

Don José Antonio started to protest, but Don Macario cut him short. "No, I understand perfectly what you mean. But it amuses me. You see, I am no longer so much in agreement with this matter of the 'God of love.' Love . . . do you think we know what God's love is? The trouble is that we have read too many romantic novels, and don't realize that the word 'love' on the lips of God has a very different meaning from when a soldier is saying sweet things to a nursemaid. God's love . . . is there anything more terrible than that?"

"Mercy cannot be terrible."

"Mercy! You always fall back on that. But, in my opinion, there is nothing more terrible than mercy, nothing more painful."

"It's a consolation to know that God forgives us."

"Mercy tranquilizes me, but does not console me. No, I tell you in all sincerity that the other life does not worry me because I may go to heaven or hell. What does frighten me is the boredom on the face of God when he sends me to one place or the other. Mercy, that is the terrible thing, to know that God is going to be weak enough to forgive us. I often think that purgatory may be just that: the shame of knowing that we are saved. Yes, the hardest thing to bear at the Last Judgment will not even be the sight of our own emptiness, but knowing that God is so good that He forgives even those of us who take advantage of that kindness of His to sneak through to salvation by the back door, thanks to His tolerance."

"The back door?"

"Yes, the back door. Because there are only two doors to heaven, the front door, which is that of sanctity, and the back door of God's tolerance. Almost none come in through the front door, but when one does God's heart rings like a bell. Many, nearly all, come in the other way, and each of these is a disappointment to Him. This idea has been running through my mind for days now. Which would be better: to let the village go on entering heaven by the back door, or to drive them to the front door? The latter is far more uncertain. This is the door of struggle, and the struggle can be lost. It is easy to get in through the back door. Often just keeping in line and not running off the rails is almost enough. As the ranks are so tight, it's almost enough to be pushed along by the crowd, the medium. But in the struggle for sanctity one is alone and naked, without any human handholds. The one who lays hold of God and can bear the heat of His presence can reach the front door. But these are very few. Most of them fall in the combat; some join the ranks of those headed for the back door; others fall still lower, to hell."

"Then do you mean that all the damned are heroes who fell?"

"No indeed. There is a back door to hell, too: that of stupidity. And it is even more frequented than that of heaven."

It was a beautiful midsummer afternoon. The sun poured in through the window, marking a rectangle on the priest's bed. The sweat trickled through the furrows on Don Macario's face. He went on: "We worry about heaven and hell as though this were exclusively our concern. In the last analysis, we are not all that important. Heaven as a personal rest home would bore me. I would prefer hell, as I prefer pain to boredom. Fortunately, heaven will be love, but in the great, consuming sense of the word. To love God, that's what matters. And it is the only happiness I desire. And I give you my word that if by suffering in hell this could be better achieved, I would prefer it."

Don José Antonio listened to all this without attempting to answer. There were moments when it seemed heresy—Jansenism, he was thinking—and others when the only difference he saw between what Don Macario was saying and what his professor of dogma had taught was that the present teacher was on the brink of death. Most people would think, and rightly so, that behind the grain of truth his words held there was a morbid exaggeration, the result of his obsessive effort to order his own thoughts.

Don Macario was a very sick man. Don Melquíades said again and again that he could not understand how he was still alive. The cancer had been spreading through his stomach, it was impossible for him to eat anything, and for over a month he had been fed only intravenously.

Don Macario went on: "But none of this can be said from the pulpit. People want to be happy even at God's expense. Oh, if God were suddenly to say that it was in hell that He was really loved, we would all change our religion. Fortunately, He cannot say that. Look, try it out one day: talk to them of hell as the place where God is not loved, but don't say a word to them about the flames, and you will see how contentedly they sit listening to you. What frightens them is the thought of real fire, not the frozen hell of not loving. It is the same with the miracles."

Don Macario had let slip this final phrase almost without realizing what he was saying, and now he regretted it. Don José Antonio looked at him without venturing a question.

Don Macario realized that an explanation was called for.

"Yes, son, the same thing holds true of miracles. No, I am not referring to the ones here—I don't even know what they were like. I am speaking in general. Men are concerned with miracles because of their effects, the legs they heal, the deaths they postpone. But the idea that when God works them He is thinking about us, this could hardly affect them less. Look, I am talking to you sincerely, the two of us here alone, as though in the confessional. I like Renato's miracles for that very reason, because they admit of no confusion. They say what is strictly necessary, and that is enough. In them one sees the hand of God—assuming that they are the work of God—though here on earth they are good for nothing. Or, rather, they are good for everything. They remind us that God has not forgotten us.

"But, as you see, what men want is the other kind. I don't know which is more miraculous, the utterance of the beatitudes or the loaves and the fishes. Naturally, people prefer the latter. The beatitudes are a real encumbrance; they don't know what to do with them, where to hide them so they will be out of the way. Haven't you noticed how little is said of the Trinity and even of the Incarnation, and how much about the Virgin of Lourdes? No, I have nothing against the appearance of the Immaculate, but I think the Virgin of Lourdes would be the first to rejoice if people talked more about the Trinity. If the miracles here served a practical purpose, you'd see how we'd have a new shrine here."

"What you mean to say is that you don't like practical miracles?"

"Indeed I do like them. Nearly all those Christ worked were of that sort. What worries me is the inversion of terms. For the fruit of the miracle to become its center, that is what frightens me. There are times when it seems to me that the fruit of the miracles is a concession God makes to human stupidity."

Don Macario moved about in his bed, and raised his hand to his head. "I'm tired," he said, "dreadfully tired."

Magdalena, too, was tired.

"You've been acting very strangely for some time, Magdalena. Is anything wrong with you?" her mother had asked as they sat down to dinner. The girl bit her lips.

"Nothing, Mama."

But now, halfway through the meal, almost without knowing what she was doing, she began to cry.

"Now I want to know what ails you." Doña Julia got up from the table.

"Nothing, Mama, it's nothing. I'm nervous, just nervous . . . I don't even know why. . . ."

"You silly little girl," her mother answered. "Some childish nonsense. Could it be that you are in love?"

The girl raised her head and looked her mother in the eye to see if there was irony in her words. She shook her head from side to side.

"You should tell me everything, child. You are very queer. You avoid me. And you spend the day in the confessional. You're not thinking of becoming a nun, are you?"

"Heavens, Mama!"

Doña Julia would have liked that. Her daughter was beginning to be a burden to her. It would have been so nice if God would take her to a convent. "Have you quarreled with one of your friends?"

"Mama, be still. Why don't you try to understand me a little?"

94

"Understand you? You see? You see how you are nothing but a child? How can I understand what I don't know?"

The clock struck half past two, and Doña Julia could not keep her eyes from straying to the window opposite Don Ricardo's house.

Magdalena understood her glance of impatience. Unable to restrain herself, she shrilled:

"Mama!"

"What is it?"

"Don't look at the window. I can't stand seeing you . . ."

"Seeing me . . . ?"

The girl lowered her head. "Nothing, Mama. Forgive me. I am so nervous. . . ."

Doña Julia shrugged her shoulders. "Definitely, I don't understand you." She went over to the girl and said, ruffling her hair: "What a bird brain!" And she laughed.

Magdalena watched her leave the dining-room and heard her humming as she changed her dress. Through the open door she could see her putting on her make-up in front of the mirror. "Mama," she called.

Without turning her head, Doña Julia answered: "What is it, daughter?"

Magdalena bit her lips. How could she say anything to a woman who attached more importance to her rouge than to her daughter? She kept quiet.

Doña Julia came back into the dining-room and took a bottle of nail polish out of a console drawer. "What were you saying, dear?"

"Nothing, Mama, it was nothing."

"I hope you won't forget to wash the dishes."

"No, Mama."

95

"I know you don't like to. But your mother's pension can't be stretched to include a cook and maid."

She was painting her nails with careful strokes of the brush. Magdalena was thinking: "I ought to tell her. Every day makes it harder."

Doña Julia was now singing the latest song hit. "He is adorable," she remarked. When she saw the girl looking at her without knowing what she was talking about, she went on: "Mario Costa, the tenor. He's got something . . . that gives you a thrill."

Magdalena was thinking: "I ought to tell her."

Doña Julia was straightening her stockings, showing her whole leg as she did so. She pulled her dress into place before the mirror. "You won't forget the dishes?"

"The dishes?"

"To wash them, I mean."

"Oh, no."

A final look in the mirror. She smiled with satisfaction. "All right, good-by, love. Be a good girl."

Magdalena was thinking: "I ought to tell her."

From the door Doña Julia called back: "Don't forget the dishes."

Magdalena cried: "Mama!"

Doña Julia came back. "Did you call me?"

Making a great effort, the girl said: "I have to . . . tell you something."

"Well, come on, tell me. Can't you see I'm in a hurry?"

Magdalena felt the tears rise to her eyes. "Mama!"

The tears were about to well over, and she hurried to speak before they choked her. She sobbed: "I'm going to have a . . . a . . ." And then the tears held back for three months overflowed.

In the street the children were playing.

"I'm Renato and you kids are the sick people."

"And I'm María Belén, who brought the bird."

"Oh, oh, my leg, cure my leg!"

"We'll kill you if you don't cure us."

"We'll kill you."

"Oh, my leg, my leg, cure my leg!"

"Oh, baby, my wife is like a bag, an old bag," Sátrapa said. "But you . . ."

Matilde laughed, stroking his bald spot. "You deserved a lot better, darling. How did you come to marry that bag of bones?"

"She was rich, you know. We were never in love. It was my father's doing. He was very foxy, and he thought that if I married her, the two biggest fortunes in the village in time would be all mine. And it wasn't a bad idea. Besides, now that I have you, that fixes everything up."

"You know that I am jealous?"

"Of my wife?" He laughed so hard that he choked.

She went on, pouting: "I wish she'd die."

He laughed again. "No such luck."

In the square the hammering of the circus-tent pegs could be heard. "What are you going to give me for the fair?" she asked.

The old woman was always sitting there at the door of the house, so dark and motionless that she might have been a wooden image. Occasionally she would say something, and it was as though she was nibbling her lips.

"Why don't they let us alone?" she would mumble.

"We've had enough. They should change nothing, not even for the better. Let things go on as they are. What do we want with miracles?"

The woman who sat sewing opposite her looked at her and made no comment. The old crone would put together a phrase and then sit silent for a long time.

"Daughter, all the sorrows have been numbered, and not one shall be spared. Neither one more nor one less. Whether we are good or bad, it's all the same. Everything is on the list."

Her little granddaughter was chasing a cat. The old woman sat watching her without a word. The minutes went by.

"What do we want with miracles? If God exists, we'll see Him when the time comes. What's the hurry? And if He doesn't . . . then we'll have a good rest underground."

The woman watched her fearfully, her eyes wide. The child had settled herself at her grandmother's feet. The old woman ran her hand over the close-cropped head, and after long meditation spoke: "Oh, child, how unlucky you are. You've got such a long time to live. And your list is still very long."

The woman moved in her chair. "Why do you say that? Why?"

The old woman sat in thought. Finally she said: "Why? There is no why. My mother told me that sorrow comes to man the way the rivers flow to the sea. Why do they go? Nobody knows, not even they. They just go. To try to understand suffering is only to increase it."

After this there was a long silence. Then the old woman shook her head and said: "Oh, God."

But her tone was so inexpressive that it was impossible

to know whether she had said: "Oh, God" or "No God."

Silence filled the room.

In the square the children were gathered around the platform that the performers had set up. It was of red and blue wood, and on the curtain a painted clown was climbing out of a chimney and two dancers were peeping archly around a curtain.

When they had put up the curtain, Santos had remarked in the tavern: "They might have painted them without the curtain."

Uncle Lucas had smiled. His pipe was out and he did not bother to light it. "I wonder what these people are thinking about. Folks are in a fine mood for jokes."

"You never can tell," Julián answered from a corner. "People have to laugh once in a while. Or they'll blow up."

Santos spoke up. "Me, I'm going. Even if it's only to see those dancers."

"Me too," Martín added.

Uncle Lucas shook his head, but said nothing. After a while he spoke: "It was with an outfit like this that Renato came."

In the square the performers went on setting up their booth.

Don José Antonio, sitting at his desk in the parish house of San Martín, was writing: "I am at a loss to understand why these things happen. This morning there were no more than sixty people in the church. Last year, when I was helping out as subdeacon, the whole village was there. I remember that Don Macario said to me: 'Everybody has come to church today. It's another act in the program. Even those who neglected to make confession during Holy Week are here; there are plenty for whom

99

this is their only visit to the church.' I ask myself if the fault is mine.

"To be sure, I have not minced my words. I have told them that sinning will get them nowhere. Perhaps I have let my anger get the best of me.

"I am discouraged, and I don't know what course to take. If I could lay the matter before the Bishop, at least that would lighten my responsibility, but as it stands, I am between the devil and the deep blue sea.

"I have been reading the entries in my diary three months back, and it makes me very sad. To think that everything was beginning to pick up and . . . But the worst of all is not knowing if this is something good or bad, not knowing whether it should be encouraged or combated. Lord, when will you take pity on me and help me to understand this?"

The clown climbed onto the platform. One eyebrow was painted white and the other red, his lower jaw black. He stepped forward and swept off his hat. The audience roared as a bird flew out of it, and went on laughing as Toni pulled at the thread by which the sparrow was fastened to his bald head. When the bird was back under the hat again, Toni said: "Good evening, gentlemen and lady men." The audience laughed. "The Pim-Pam-Pum Circus has the great honor"—and he ran from one side of the stage to the other—"of presenting to you tonight's preformance"—the audience laughed at the pronunciation. "I am the clown, as you can see. And you probably want to know what I am called. Well, I am not called. I come without calling."

Trini, Doña Asunción's maid, doubled up with laughter. "Oh, isn't he funny!" And she repeated this over and over until finally Roque, her sweetheart, got mad. Though he had been in a bad humor to start with because, in his opinion, there was too much light in the square.

Renato twisted in his bed. He was thinking: "I have to hang on to this happiness at all costs. Because it's all I've got left. And nobody has a right to take it from me. They can take my peace, but not my happiness. If they do, I might as well be dead. Couldn't they try to understand me a little? You made a mistake when you chose me. I was born for this: to juggle six balls and send the trains through. Miracles are a priest's business. Don José Antonio. Or any other one. To think that a few months ago I was happy . . . I'll have to leave the village. . . ."

The clown went on with his patter: "As I was saying, this circus is called the Pim-Pam-Pum Circus because it is like a pistol. As soon as you get in front of it you die— laughing."

"Oh, isn't he funny!" Trini repeated.

"It has a special effect on mothers-in-law."

Trini couldn't hear the last word because even Roque laughed.

Magdalena was making signs from the window. "Come around to the back. The back door. I've got the key." In a minute she was in Rodrigo's arms. "She knows."

"Had she noticed?"

"No, I told her."

"What happened?"

Magdalena began to cry.

"What did she say?"

"It was awful." The girl pressed tighter against him as

though seeking protection. "She was like a wild thing. Look," and she showed him her neck, "Look at that scratch."

"The bitch! Did you tell her we want to get married?"

"She wouldn't listen to me. She said it would be a scandal. That I am just a child. That I had to . . ."

"What?"

"That I had to . . ."

"No!"

"I told her I wouldn't. That rather than that . . ."

A roar of laughter came from the square.

". . . that rather than that . . ."

Another roar, louder than the first.

". . . that rather than that I would hang myself."

Rodrigo's arms tightened around her as though both of them had to defend themselves from someone. From the plaza came the applause with which the entrance of the dancers was greeted. "Why can't they let us be happy?" The sounds of the saxophone filled the village. The two girls began to sway to the shouts of the spectators. Magdalena said: "My mother said it was a horrible sin." As the dancers twirled, their skirts looked like bells. "A sin . . ." Rodrigo repeated. A phrase shouted in the plaza was followed by lewd laughter. "Don't you think God would be more understanding than your mother? It's a greater sin to have an abortion." The two dancers came down among the audience, and coppers were thrown into the baskets they held. "She doesn't think that is a sin." The dancers laughed as the village lads jostled them. "They're going to make life impossible for us. We would be so happy with our . . ." The saxophone struck up a new tune. One of the women was singing in a hot, crooning voice. "Couldn't we run away?" Magdalena asked.

"Anywhere." The woman was singing: "The first time we met . . ." "They'd send the police after us." ". . . and you held me in your sweet arms," the song went on. "We are alone, Magdalena. Alone against the whole world." The words of the song could no longer be made out. The clock struck one.

◆◆◆◆◆◆◆◆◆◆

8   Don Melquíades had said: "I think that . . . that . . ."

Don Macario finished the sentence for him: ". . . that this is about over." And they all noticed how his face contracted in pain. For a long time he remained silent, and then, his eyes open to their full width, he asked: "How much time have I left?"

Don Melquíades looked at him in surprise. "I am not God to say. Perhaps days, hours, weeks . . ."

Don Macario drew a deep breath. "Leave me alone," he said.

Marta controlled her sobs, but tears streamed down her face. "Shall I send for Don José Antonio?"

There was a long pause before Don Macario answered. "Tomorrow." And then, nervously: "Now leave me alone."

Don Melquíades left, unable to understand that coldness, so different from the reaction he had expected.

The priest called out: "Marta! Hand me the crucifix."

Marta closed the door, and Don Macario clasped the crucifix between his hands until they hurt. He turned his face to the wall, which seemed to him blinding white and bare. "That is what my life has been like," he thought, "white, but completely empty." And then: "If at least I had been granted a painful death. But God has punished me by sending me the death I deserve, a stupid death that comes without my feeling it." He broke out in a cold, clammy sweat. "Perhaps I haven't lived. I have been a puppet full of sawdust, nothing more." He sat up in bed and rested his head against the wall. "To live, to live." He sobbed. And then, as if seized by a convulsive laugh: "I'm dying. That poor fool of a doctor! You have to be alive to die." Without knowing what he was doing he sat up, his feet on the floor. The bright moonlight traced the eight panes of the window on the floor. He had to lean on the table to stand up. "You have to be alive," he said.

The glass of the window was cold against his forehead. The plaza was empty.

"The kingdom of death," he said. "You alone lived, God, and You have gone. All below zero. Useless." Now he was shouting.

Marta called from the door: "Is anything the matter, Macario?"

The priest had the impression that someone had called him. But he did not move.

"Macario, Macario, did you call me?"

But he was thinking: "Nobody, there is nobody in the plaza," and he did not hear the footsteps withdraw. "Below zero," he repeated. The plashing of the fountain in the square could be heard. A dog barked. "The whole village has cancer. And doesn't know it." He brushed away the sweat that was running down his forehead. "My heart is emptier than this plaza. And perhaps the worst is that

You have no right to send me to hell unless You have another hell of cold, a terrible emptiness between heaven and the real hell. There, forever condemned to carry out meticulously a clutch of paltry duties. Or a desert. To walk, walk, walk. Without seeing anybody. Or seeing people without seeing them, like here."

His legs were buckling. He felt very weak. "To love," he was thinking. He shook his head. "Too much . . ." Now he felt more rested, though he was not aware that it was because his body had slipped to the floor and his head was resting beside the overturned wastepaper basket.

"Happy . . . only then was I happy. But how return now to that lost infancy?" Once again he was by the village fountain, a child whipping the water with a stick and then running from the scolding women. His face was wet with sweat, and he tried to raise a hand to lash the cool water. But where was the fountain, where had it gone? And youth, stupid, never-understood youth? "It's a bored man who is coming to you, Christ."

He felt an intense cold such as he had never known before. "Days, hours, perhaps weeks," Don Melquíades shouted, mounted in a pulpit. And his spiritual father, old Don Rafael, was feeling his pulse: "My children, you must be saints. Man was created to praise and serve God. Each and every one of you, hearken to what I am saying, each and every one of you has the duty to be a saint." How far off were the years he had spent in the obscure seminary. To be a saint . . . The word had seemed too big to him.

Now he felt an oppression around his heart. He saw the rector of the seminary approaching, laughing his loud, brusque laugh. Then he suddenly grew serious and shouted: "Said the Holy Ghost: As you are neither hot nor cold I shall spew you from my mouth. Remember those words," and Don Macario raised his supplicating eyes and saw how his heart swelled and emptied like a bladder filled with blood as the rector laughed and squeezed it harder and harder.

Now his mother had his heart between her hands: "Son, you must be good, good, good." Her hair was completely white, and she smiled as she saw her son in his vestments, as though this of itself assured his entry into heaven.

"When my feet, at the hour of death, know that their course . . ." Don Macario was no longer sure whether he had feet or not. He had the feeling that he no longer existed from the waist down. He tried to imagine his body cut off at the middle. He wanted to laugh at his dream, but when he tried to raise his head to convince himself of the absurdity of his delirium, he could no longer move it. He tried to stretch out his right hand, but it was clutching a metal object he could not identify. His fingers were clenched around metal.

"What frightens me is God's grief at sending me to heaven or to hell. God," he said, "God," and he felt that he was already before Him. At first He was like a statue with blank eyes, like the Greek statues in the museums. Little by little his eyes began to emerge, and to grow and grow until the statue was all eyes, and they went on growing until they had filled the Judgment Hall.

Don Macario pressed his head against the floor. But the eyes went on growing, and suddenly they turned into a sea of tiny, small eyes, a sea that ran into his mouth, producing nausea. He pressed his forehead against the floor until it hurt, and the nails of his left hand sank into the wood. "A few hours, only a few hours," Don Melquíades shouted.

And Don Macario answered: "I will go, wherever it may be, though there is only a minute left, I will go, I will go." He tried to get up, but fell heavily to the floor, striking his head, and lay motionless.

The moon, which had been hidden behind a cloud, now flooded the room, tracing on the poor body a square of milky light divided by the gratings of shadows of the balcony, which crossed it like the bars of prison.

When at two o'clock in the morning Marta entered her brother's room to ask him how he felt, she found him lying face down at the foot of the window. The poor woman, without venturing to touch him, ran into the street screaming and began to hammer madly at Don Melquíades's door. Several windows were thrown open and behind them the frightened faces of the neighbors appeared.

"No, he's not dead," Don Melquíades said.

They lifted him carefully to his bed. "He's had a collapse . . . he may not come out of it." And there came the sound of convulsive weeping.

But Don Macario did recover consciousness.

"José Antonio, my son," he murmured as he saw by his bedside the young priest with the box holding the oils of the Extreme Unction hanging from his neck. At his side Don Melquíades stood frowning, and Juanele, the altar boy, sweating from rushing on his bicycle for the priest. From the farther wall came the choked sobs of Marta and the twins.

Don Macario looked from one to another of the group. Then he asked, as though already in the other world: "Didn't Renato come?"

"Renato? Why should he come?"

Don Macario made a gesture as though he, in turn, did not understand the question. "Tell him to come, I want him to come." And then: "Now leave us alone."

When the others had gone out, Don Macario indicated the bed with his eyes, saying to Don José Antonio: "Sit down. Here. That's right."

The old priest's eyes reflected the fatigue of a long struggle, and they were still filmed with anxiety, though perhaps happiness was faintly breaking through.

"I am afraid, my son, I am terribly afraid," he said. "It has been a dreadful night. I have seen my life minute by minute, as though I were living it over again . . . and it has been terrible. Almost as though I had already been through the Judgment. The eyes of Christ, the eyes of all the men who have lived, besieged me. It was as though you had been ordered to eat a basket of filberts, but knew beforehand that they were all hollow, and still went on cracking them in the secret hope that there might be one, just one, that was good, but there wasn't any. And feeling, with all this, that every sterile minute you called up was laughing at you, that your very entrails were guffawing. And then you understood that you deserved to be damned, and that instead of doing it, they were cruelly drawing out the pronouncement of sentence, but telling you beforehand that there was no appeal. Can you understand that kind of hell?"

No, Don José Antonio understood nothing. He looked at the old priest with wide, startled eyes. He felt he must say something. "But God knows that you don't deserve to be damned."

Don Macario turned a devastatingly gray look upon him. "How little that consoles me! If it was a question of sins, I would know that everything was very simple. You would raise your hand and everything would be over. But it is much worse than that, my son; all your absolutions cannot return to me one minute of all those I have lost. And the glory I should have given to God, and failed to give, will be lost for all the ages to come. How can I return to Christ's veins the blood that was uselessly shed? I had a mission: to fill all the hours of my life with fire. Now those hours will go rattling throughout eternity, rattling emptily about me, and nobody, not even God, can fill them with meaning. Do you call that heaven?"

Don Macario moved restlessly in his bed. His breathing was becoming more labored every minute. "I do not know if I should say these things to you, but I know that I must not go without saying them to someone."

He took Don José Antonio by the hand and drew him toward him. His eyes shone as though he was about to cry. "I have not understood God in my whole life. I have spent years and years talking about Him, but without knowing Him. I was talking about a puppet, about a sorry creature I had invented, of my own size. A being one could like and respect, but not love or serve. So that people would understand Him, I made him small, without realizing that a God that can fit into a human head is no kind of a God. I talked about His law, but not about Him. I took Him in my hands because in our senselessness we do even that: saying a few words and thinking that we have between our hands the body and the blood of the little God we have invented, and that the great God comes, the only one that exists, the only one worth while to exist."

At this point he stopped. Don José Antonio noticed that the skeletal palm of his hand grew tense against his. Then he went on: "For only six months have I known God. It was the day Don Melquíades told me . . . that I was going." He stopped again. He was talking convulsively.

Don José Antonio thought he was going to burst into tears. "Calm yourself," he said.

"Calm myself? What for? Perhaps by daybreak I will be calmed once and for all. Listen to me and try to understand." He was almost shouting. "These have been six horrible months, understanding God and lacking the courage to love Him. He always closing in on me with maddening clarity, and I putting Him off. Ah, I could not have endured six months of sanctity."

Don José Antonio felt Don Macario's whole body shudder as he pronounced this word. He started to say something. But the old man broke in: "Yes, let me pronounce that word: sanctity. For six months it has tormented me. Do you know what it is to go after your eyes have been opened? What a tragedy not to be blind, not to be able to be blind! It is only love that can fill men's lives. And in my life, not one act of love!"—these last words were a scream.

"So many Masses," the young priest said hesitantly.

"Oh, God!"

A long silence followed. The clock struck the hour of three.

"So many Masses . . ." Don Macario's eyes shone as though he was on the point of tears. "So many Masses . . ."

Don José Antonio expected him to burst out crying, but it was as though some power was holding a check-rein on the tears. At that moment there was a knock at the street door. Marta came into the room.

"It's Renato."

Don Macario turned his head quickly. "Tell him to come in."

He said the words faintly, and Don José Antonio felt the chill hand in his relax.

"Tell him to come in."

Renato loomed in the doorway. There was a strange smile on his lips which disconcerted Don José Antonio. The young priest withdrew a few paces to watch the scene; for the first time, after all that had occurred, those two men had come together. The young priest had the impression that Renato had aged in those months. He had many gray hairs, but his gaze had become luminous and his corduroy clothes had a different air. Renato approached the bed and took the place Don José Antonio had just left. The latter stood at the foot of the bed. Don Macario and Renato looked at each other without talking. To the young priest these seconds seemed eternal.

Don Macario seemed to pay no attention to Renato, and was back at his obsessions. He put his hand between those of the switchman, and repeated: "So many Masses!"

And then the tears came, gentle tears that hung for a moment on his eyelids and then rolled off onto the pillow. Renato pressed the bony hand in silence. Don José Antonio realized that the switchman was crying, too. But he could not have said whose tears had begun first.

9 Manuela listened intently. There was no doubt about it, they were ringing. She shook her husband by the shoulder: "Lucio, Lucio, wake up!"

The sacristan grunted and turned over.

"Lucio, wake up! Can't you hear them ringing?"

The sacristan grunted again. "It's still early."

She took him by both shoulders and shook him hard: "I tell you they are ringing the bells."

"The bells? Ringing the bells? Who?"

"That's what I am trying to tell you."

Lucio now sat up in bed. "It can't be."

"Just listen."

"You're right. What time is it?"

"It's not four yet."

"Four? I don't understand. And they're ringing for Mass. At this hour."

"Come on."

"All right, let's go."

Still only half dressed, Lucio and Manuela went out into the street. Windows were being opened to right and left.

"What's the matter?"

"We don't know; we're going to see."

There was no doubt about it: someone was ringing the bells, and, besides, someone who knew how. The peal was perfect: tan, tan, tan, tan-tan-tan. Perfect. Lucio felt in his pocket for the key to the bell tower, the only one in the village.

They hurried through the streets as though the devil was after them, and in the plaza two women joined them. "Maybe they've broken down the door."

But the door was intact and locked. They started up the stairs, which seemed steeper than ever. For a moment the three women were afraid and stopped.

Lucio called to them: "Aren't you coming?"

Impelled by a strange courage, they climbed on. There was nobody on the second floor, but they could clearly see the ropes moving.

"Come on, come on!"

They continued their ascent. All four were panting. Lucio was the first to reach the platform. "Oh!" He stopped at the door. Six eyes peered over his shoulder.

"There's no one."

"No one."

"A miracle."

And the four stood shivering there on the stairs while the bells, rung by invisible hands, swung back and forth, back and forth.

It was Manuela who spoke: "Renato."

The early morning breeze blew gentle and cool.

Renato had said: "What can you expect of children except to get themselves dirty?"

Don Macario had taken one of his hands and pressed it hard. "But I have seen God, you understand? The others . . . What do they really know of God? But we . . . I have no right to disappoint God. The Saints . . ."

113

"The saints . . . Don't you believe that it was the saints who achieved their sanctity. At the hour of truth we all go in by the front door—of mercy."

Don José Antonio asked himself how it was that Renato was saying this when he had not heard their dialogue days before.

"But I . . ." Don Macario said.

"Don't talk so much about yourself. That may be pride. Perhaps . . ." He paused.

Don Macario raised his eyes. "Speak, speak without fear. You don't know the good you are doing me. I need truth more than life. You were saying . . ."

"That perhaps you are more frightened by the thought that it is you who are disappointing God than by the idea of God's disappointment."

Don Macario opened his eyes as though a flood of light had suddenly come over them. Of painful light.

Renato stopped short, laughing. "I don't know why I am talking this nonsense. But I do think you ought to be happy to go to the Father's house."

"But I am afraid. I am afraid just because he is the Father. If he were only a judge, he would punish me, and that would be that. But he is a Father. Believe me, Renato, if there were a third way between life and death, I would choose it for myself. I don't want to live because now I would have no choice but to be a saint. And I lack the courage. But neither do I dare to die, because the Judgment terrifies me. Oh, if only annihilation were possible."

"I don't know what this is. But I cannot understand your fear. At the Judgment, I believe that if He finds only a single penny He will make up the balance, which will always be a lot. I don't know how, but He will make it up. And here, on this earth, there is always time to be good."

"Time . . ."

"Yes, there's always time. A second is enough to say: 'I love You.'"

"And what about the rest of life?"

Renato shook his head. He pointed to the window. "The trees give fruit in the summer. If one winter all of a sudden they should begin to think, they would all commit suicide. Oh, yes, it would be wonderful if they gave fruit in all the four seasons, but . . ."

"Give fruit . . ." Don Macario's face contracted painfully. It was as dry as parchment. "Listen to me. Last night I looked out of the window and the whole village was cancerous. There's not one sound person. That is my life. Thirty years corrupting this village." He was gesticulating nervously with his right hand.

Renato pressed it between his. "Now, you listen to me. You think María is cancerous? Then why hasn't she left Sátrapa? And what about Nicolás, who did not utter a word of blasphemy when his wife died? And wasn't Pilar an angel? And Sito and María Belén? And what about those who sin and weep for their sins?"

The first smile began to play around Don Macario's lips. He complained like a child: "But what I might have done . . ."

"You have not been a saint. And it grieves you that you are not. Perhaps that in itself is enough, don't you think?" The first streaks of light were showing through the window. "We are all children in the sight of God. You will soon be in His arms and He will sing a lullaby so you will fall asleep and forget all this hurly-burly."

"Thank you," said Don Macario. And he became quiet.

Renato had bowed his head as though he, too, felt himself lulled by God.

115

Don Macario looked up. "Renato."

"What?"

"Tell me, aren't you afraid of God? Swear to me that you are at ease, that you do not fear Him."

"Of course I fear Him. Naturally, I am afraid of Him."

"And are you at ease?"

"Yes, for that very reason, because I am afraid. One must suffer, one always has to suffer."

"Do you suffer?"

"Of course. That's why I am happy. For the last months I have been happier than ever before, and it's because of that, because I suffer more than ever before. Do you understand?"

"But doesn't God burn you?"

"I know nothing about theology, Father, but I think he does. Otherwise, how could I be so happy?"

The silence that followed was long.

"Renato, I need to ask a favor of you."

"What is it?"

"I would like to say a Mass."

Renato looked at him without understanding. "And what do you want me to do?" he asked.

"Renato," Don Macario said, clasping his hand, "we have not talked about you, about your things. As you can imagine, they have told me all about it."

"But that is water over the dam, Father. That is finished and done with. I'd rather not talk about it."

"Renato." The priest's hands were trembling. "I need a miracle. I need a miracle. To say one Mass and then die. I would like my life to leave a good taste in God's mouth."

Renato's gaze grew more transparent than ever. He shook his head. "Impossible. I don't know. Then . . . ask it of God. But know this: miracles are nothing but something additional; at bottom they are of no use for what we hope for. There are so many miracles: living, loving God, serving Him. Those . . ."

"But I need to say Mass." The tears were welling up again in the old man's eyes.

Renato laid his hand on Don Macario's head and caressed it as though he were a child. "This is your Mass," he said, "dying. And doing it without any fuss. Carrying out the will of the Father and not your own. Renouncing an elegant death—that is your Mass. The one that will leave a good taste in His mouth."

Don Macario raised his head. "You think . . ." He shifted his body nervously. ". . . that this . . ." His whole body was trembling. ". . . that this . . ." His eyes gleamed like those of a man who has discovered the answer to a problem. ". . . is enough?"

Renato did not speak. He nodded in assent. Don Macario's eyes raised ceilingward. Again he took Renato's hand and pressed it hard. "Thank . . ." he said. A sudden trembling seized him, and he fell back heavily on the pillow.

Renato called out, and Don Melquíades hurried into the room.

"Quick. An injection. He's going."

Don Macario stirred. "Yes, I am going," he said without opening his eyes. And he went on: "I will approach the altar of God and you will see how the fruit of the tree ripens."

"His mind is wandering," Don Melquíades said. Renato had gone down on his knees. Don José Antonio opened the window, through which glimmers of light were coming. Don Melquíades stood over the dying man with the syringe in his hand, but he stopped short, for at that moment the bells began to ring. The doctor and the priest looked at one another.

"Are those the bells?"

"Yes."

"Is that the death knell?"

"No, they are calling to Mass."

"I don't understand it."

"Neither do I."

Don Macario went on in his delirium: "Judge me, Lord, for You know that I love You. Like the children in the yard who are always thirsty, it must be true that we are all blind. You understand, don't You? As though there were a fire . . . I'm tired of playing, it's over; me sinner, *beatam Mariam semper virginem;* we can go out in the yard if you like . . . Marta, did the mail come? Tell Mama to wait for . . . *misereatur tui Omnipotens Deus.* All right, my son, do not sin again. We men offend God, dear brethren, and the prayers of the breviary are never finished. I need a miracle. And the Epistle? There is no Epistle in this Missal. *Sanctus, Sanctus, Sanctus.* Fire . . . this house is on fire . . . *Hoc est* . . . Oh, how thirsty I am. *Sanguis, Sanguis.* Tell me, please, do you suffer? Do you suffer much? *Effundetur. Ef-fun-de-tur.* I am forgetting everything, even Latin. How I would love to return to the seminary. This vacation is too long. Jesus Christ of my death, You are a child. . . ."

With every moment the light was growing brighter. All the village was up now, awakened by the bells that went on ringing, and many of the people had gathered before the parish house.

"Open the windows. I want to see if it is summer. *Agnus, agnus Dei* . . ."

The room was filling up with people who listened in the

tensest silence. Don Macario went on talking, but now only occasional words could be made out. Don José Antonio did not venture to read the commendation of the soul because he did not want to break the silence, and because it was useless: Don Macario could no longer hear anything of this world. He stopped talking for a moment. He breathed heavily, and then mumbled a phrase in which only these broken words could be made out: "*Missa est . . . spring . . . give me . . . the hoop . . . the hoop . . .*"

At that moment the bells in the tower stopped ringing. Renato got to his feet and laid his hand on the priest's forehead. "Tell the sacristan to ring the death knell."

It was ten on Saturday morning when, in the direction of the Colina de las Angustias, the first cloud in four months loomed up. The whole village looked toward the hill, and a smile was born in many eyes. The earth was hard and dry, and the wagons going by raised a dust that dried all the throats of the village. The sun was hot and stormy, and men and the earth dreamed of rain. It soon was seen that that cloud was not the only one. A number of white clouds edged in purple were scudding toward the village. By eleven the whole sky was covered with clouds, still clear, but slowly growing darker.

The dinner hour was a happy one in every house. At any minute the crash would be heard, and then the longed-for water.

At four o'clock the bells of Torre were tolling. It was the hour of Don Macario's burial. The villagers had spent the whole previous day watching over the corpse, and the funeral was awaited like some special event, as always happens on the death of a priest in the villages.

"It looks to me as though we would get drenched at the funeral."

"Just so it rains I don't mind being drenched ten days together."

The people had gathered around the parish house. There were women crying and children running about happily. The thuds of the hammer putting together the coffin could be heard in the street. But the talk was of nothing but the rain.

The box that was Don Macario's final resting-place was black and gold. Someone said: "They have dressed him as though he were going to say Mass."

"He looks as though he were smiling."

"Poor soul."

The heavy tread of the four men bearing the coffin could be heard coming down the stairs. And at the very moment the corpse appeared at the door a flash of lightning lit up the sky. It was a dry, jagged flash, like a whiplash.

"There it comes!"

And a loud, prolonged reverberation of thunder was accompanied by a gallery of rustic smiles.

A swift wind sprang up and brought hands to eyes. The whorls of dust were blinding. Several claps of thunder similar to the first followed still closer on the lightning flashes.

"Don't ring the bells," someone said. "It might frighten off the clouds."

Renato had gone up to the Colina de las Angustias, which stood solitary. He wanted to see the funeral, but lacked courage to mingle with the people. He had been told that the previous morning the bells had rung of themselves, and everybody had laughed when he swore that he had not heard them. He would never understand. Why did such things happen? What useful purpose was served by the bells ringing of themselves? If it were a question of a miracle, why not grant Don Macario the pleasure of dying while officiating at Mass? This was what Manuela had asked, and Renato felt that she was right; but the fact remained that he had had no hand in the business. He had not asked for a miracle of one kind or another; all he had done was to pray. And now everyone was agape over this strange fruit. It was as though you planted an apple tree and it brought forth watering-cans. There was no question about it, God was making him look like a fool.

It was at that moment that the first roll of thunder came. "How I wish it would rain," Renato said to himself. He was afraid to intimate to God what he wanted. "I feel so sorry for the village. How wonderful it would be if . . ."

Down the Calle de las Monjas came the vanguard of the procession. First, several rows of children winding along, then the altar boys, their red robes giving a note of color to the leaden afternoon. When the black casket, carried on the shoulders of four village youths, appeared, Renato could not have said whether the emotion he felt was happiness or sadness.

"Lord, You know he loved You," he said. "He was a boy who was trying to be a man. Now he is in his place. And he will know what peace is, Your sorrowful peace."

The procession moved along, almost hidden in the cloud of dust. Renato could sense the hundreds of heads raised toward a sky that never quite broke into rain. "Lord," he almost shouted. "It should rain; try to understand, it should rain." Then he was frightened at what he had just said, and added: "If it is possible."

The gate of the cemetery swung back, and the procession began to disappear behind it as though into a huge maw. At that moment Renato felt a great sense of loneliness. As though a few square inches of the small plot of earth still under his feet had been taken away.

A long flash of lightning crossed the sky from horizon to horizon, followed by a clap of thunder as though the whole earth had cracked, which made Renato cover his ears. Although he did not know that the thunder had coincided with the thud of the first clod of dirt on Don Macario's coffin, the switchman said: "Now."

And at the same time as he, four hundred throats down there in the cemetery had said the same thing.

But at that very moment a wind of gale strength sprang up, and the suffering eyes of all the villagers of Torre saw a great blue swath begin to open up in the sky as the clouds, like another hurried procession, swept away from the village.

There were curses on every lip, and many spat on the ground and then stepped on their spittle. Renato, off on the Colina de las Angustias, shook his head from right to left and watched the procession, confused and disorderly, make its way back to the village amid clouds of dust.

By six in the afternoon the sky was as tense as a drumhead; not a cloud was visible for miles around.

10

That night almost nobody slept in Torre. The conviction that it was not going to rain had settled on every heart.

The old woman had said: "It was written." And then after a long silence: "The writings of God are not erased with tears."

The women looked at their men fearfully. They could read in their eyes dejection's total victory. At other times they had cursed or shouted. Today not one of them said a word. They mechanically swallowed their dinners with the vacant expression of oxen. Then they went to bed without saying a word. The only gesture that had identified them as living beings had been a nervous caress to the children when they came to kiss them good-night. The women confined their weeping to their pillows. They knew only too well that the least spark might fire the barrels of hate.

Perhaps the eyes most charged with hate that night were those of Sátrapa. He had been happy the day before, thinking that a good rain could still save the acres of grapes he owned between Torre and Marzales. A good vintage would make up for the failure of the grains. At least it would pay for the seed. But now he saw that it was to be total disaster. And this meant a loss of many thousands.

He did not even feel like going to see Matilde. He sat

down alone with a bottle of cognac and spent the afternoon adding up figures and drinking steadily.

Sátrapa was no devil, but simply what people call a sharp customer. He knew perfectly well which card to play at every trick, and once he had made up his mind, he put his whole soul into the game and knew no scruples.

Fat and shiny, his face was always wreathed in smiles. Looking at him, one could not help wondering if it was true that in the long run the evil were always cast down. For the fact is that, on the human plane, everything worked out to his advantage. Except for a son. Yes, that had gone wrong. And it had been the great illusion of his life.

He could still remember his nervous pacing of the kitchen where María's labored breathing could be heard. They had not been married even a year. To be sure, he had never really loved her, but he felt that from the day on which she would make him a father, he might begin to. Perhaps she was too good for him, with her unvarying submission, like a servant, even like a martyr.

His son would be called César, like himself. What a good-looking lad he would be. And the satisfaction of putting into his hands the biggest fortune in the village, which included nearly everything the eye could see. He would even give him the nickname he had inherited from his own father, "Sátrapa." He savored the word like the most illustrious of patronymics.

The midwife came hurriedly out of the bedroom.

"Has anything gone wrong?"

"No, everything is going well." And the woman disappeared up the stairs.

Sátrapa was now remembering every detail with photographic recall. How he had wanted to go into the room

124

where his wife was moaning, and how Don Melquíades had blocked the door. "No, you can't go in."

The midwife had gone back in with a bundle under her arm.

"But what is the matter?"

"Now, don't get nervous. Nothing is going to happen."

He closed the door just as María gave a scream. Then the panting. Then silence. Sweating, Sátrapa huddled against the door, stepping out his cigarette with his foot. "She's dead," he thought, and he realized that he was beginning to love his wife.

The door opened and Don Melquíades said: "At last."

"Is she dead?"

"No. It's a girl."

Sátrapa raised a hand to his sweating forehead. "A girl?"

"Yes."

Don Melquíades went back into the room and closed the door. Sátrapa was disappointed; he had expected something different. Someone at his side said: "It's always best to start with a girl."

"Maybe you're right."

It was a quarter of an hour before Don Melquíades came out again.

"You can give thanks to God."

"What . . . ?"

"It's a miracle that María is alive. It was a hard delivery, and I am afraid the child may be a little deformed."

A wave of hate toward his wife welled up in Sátrapa. He asked himself why, without being able to explain it to himself. He did not understand it until the next day, when the doctor told him that this would be his wife's last delivery. Then Sátrapa felt himself definitively separated from María. Moreover, the girl's deformity became more pronounced as she grew older. At first it had been only that the left leg was twisted and shorter than the right. But, probably as a result of that uneven gait, the deformity had twisted her back until finally it became definitely humped. The girl's face, too, seemed prematurely aged, with the long nose drooping over the lips. Only María Belén's eyes were beautiful: small and bright, they had sparkle and transparence that illuminated everything they rested on. But Sátrapa was not the best person to appreciate the purity of a glance.

And so he had begun to withdraw from his home. At first his visits to the capital were more frequent than they should have been. And now Matilde.

That frustration of the hoped-for son had changed him, too, in money matters. What before had been a legitimate desire to provide for his son's future had turned into a sordid ambition to make himself master of the village. He was not a miser, nor did he even care about having more or less money; his one desire was to have more than anyone else, to know that when the chips were down everyone would have to turn to him.

For that reason his attitude toward what was happening in the village was completely different from that of anyone else—from that of Uncle Lucas, for example. To be sure, he was the one who stood to lose the most from the drought, but the miracles hurt him more than the lack of rain. The worst was not the loss of the wheat, but seeing that Renato had taken his place as the center of the village. What especially hurt him was the humiliation he had suffered the day of the raising of the cross.

Try as he would, he could not forget it. He saw himself kneeling before Renato, enduring his insults without knowing what to answer. What had happened to him?

Why had he failed to react at the moment? He recalled the sleepless night he had spent, trying during the long hours to think up an answer, the answer he should have given that afternoon, and being unable to do so. He had delved in his memory for something to throw up to Renato, but had found nothing. And it was then that he made his great discovery, which would make him hate Renato as long as he lived: the realization that the switchman was the only person in the village who had never depended on him, who had never asked him for the smallest favor. This was enough to make him feel dethroned, the fact that there was someone in Torre who lived as though he, Sátrapa, did not exist.

What he had desired with his whole soul that night was that Renato should have to turn to him for something. He would have given his entire fortune just to see Renato on his knees before him, asking a favor of him, any kind of favor, even if nothing more than a match to light a cigarette. He would give anything, even his life, if Renato asked for it, but first he would make him grovel, he would spit on him.

This was what he had thought the night of the miracle of the cross. Now he cursed him anew, for that dreamed-of opportunity had arisen and he had not known how to take advantage of it. It was on the occasion of the medicines for Pilar. Why had he not realized his dreams that day? Renato had come to him, humbly begging a few pesetas. Sátrapa cursed himself for having refused so quickly. He had practically chased him out of the house without looking at him. The trouble was that in front of Renato he felt defeated, inhibited, and his momentary wrath had been merely a device to hide his panic.

Now he realized that each day Renato was becoming

more and more the focal point of the village, that on every occasion the thoughts of his neighbors turned toward the switchman. It was not money the people wanted, but wonders. Even if he had flung open the doors of his house, the village would have kept going to Renato to ask for miracles.

"I don't know myself," he thought. "I am old. I am getting old."

And he began to feel a need to display his strength. It gave him satisfaction to insult his wife. It warmed his heart to see Don Sebastián in a lather, that mayor he had had appointed just because he was the weakest, most easily managed man in the village. And he squeezed his debtors at the same time that he flaunted his own extravagance.

One day Matilde was wearing a new gold watch, and the whole village commented on it.

"He's bought her a gold watch."

"He's bought her a gold watch."

"He's bought her a gold watch."

Another day the new threshing machine made its appearance in the village, a threshing machine that was perfectly useless that year, but was a way of letting everyone know that he was still powerful.

"I'm going to buy it if I have to pawn my soul," he had decided.

And when the farmers came to ask for a loan, he put on his pleasantest smile. He invited them into his office, which was completely out of place in the house of a farmer, and which he had furnished in a way to impress the rustics. He asked them to sit down in one of the oversize armchairs into which the poor devils sank awkwardly. He slowly lighted a cigar, and took a long puff. And then he asked: "How much?"

When they answered: "Well, now, you see, with this business of Renato . . ." he realized that all his display was useless, that his money wasn't worth a cent, and that even when the villagers knelt begging before him, their thoughts were on Renato.

That was why Sátrapa could not sleep. He gritted his teeth and said: "He has to be got rid of. I don't care how."

Nor could Magdalena sleep that night. She had never been so nervous. She could not sort out so many ideas. She had sent a message to Rodrigo: "Tonight at two. At the back door."

There was no choice. If she was still in the house the next morning, everything would be over for her. Her mother had said: "Tomorrow we go to the capital."

She had not said what for, but Magdalena understood perfectly. Her mother had been very worried during the preceding days, and had made two telephone calls to Irola. "I think . . . she wants to get rid of this and then put me in a boarding school."

Rodrigo had flushed with anger. "I'll kill her first." And then, calmer, had said: "We'll run away; there's nothing else for us to do." She had nodded.

She caressed the life she bore within her. "They wanted to kill you," she said, almost out loud. And she felt her eyes fill with tears. The clock struck eleven. Could she stay awake until two? Her mother slept in the front room and would not hear her go into the back yard.

It was a bright night with an almost full moon shining in the sky. "What will we do in Madrid?" Magdalena wondered. She had very little money. She had her father's gold watch, three silver spoons, and her earrings. "How much will they bring?" Rodrigo probably had a little money, too. "The most important thing is to save you," she said to the child is her womb. The minutes seemed interminable.

Things were going worse with Rodrigo, and Magdalena would have suffered if she had known the truth. The boy was nineteen and in his second year of law at the University of Valladolid. He was the oldest of eight children, and during the summer he spent several months with an uncle who helped his brother out with the bringing up of that regiment. He had met Magdalena in church the previous summer, and they had corresponded, sending the letters through a friend, all the past year. This summer they had taken advantage of Doña Julia's frequent visits to Don Ricardo's house to meet. Rodrigo would have preferred a normal courtship, but that afternoon when the girl had flung herself into his arms he had lost his head. Now he was in a constant state of anxiety, particularly since she had told him she was pregnant. There were moments when he told himself he hated her; at others, he would have died for her. When he was with her he loved her with a tenderness that was almost paternal; when he was away from her, he would have liked to flee the village and never hear of her again if his sense of decency had not restrained him.

That night, after dinner, his uncle had taken him to his room. "Look here, Rodrigo, what ails you? For a month you have been acting as though you were feeble-minded."

Rodrigo had told him everything, and his uncle had slapped him until he was worn out, and then had pushed him into the closet and locked it.

"Whatever has the boy done?" he heard his aunt ask.

"You mind your own business," his uncle had shouted at her.

Rodrigo, tearstained and shaken up by the beating, had fallen on a trunk and then had not known what to do. The wildest ideas flitted through his mind, with the thought of suicide uppermost. He felt almost like a character in a romantic drama.

Finally he hit on a much more prosaic solution as the result of finding a box half full of bottles of cognac in the closet. He hated cognac, but it occurred to him that the only way to get to sleep would be to get drunk. He had to push the cork into the bottle after breaking it up with a nail. The first swallow—full of bits of cork—burned his mouth and throat. He went on drinking it as though it was a physic.

"Forgive me, Magdalena," he said out loud.

He tried to imagine what the girl would do when two o'clock came and he did not arrive. He went on drinking. He felt happy and laughed at his suicide plans. "I would have had to leave a letter for the judge." He took another drink. "It's too bad. There's no paper here."

By the time it struck twelve the bottle was half empty. Rodrigo was asleep on the trunk with a folded blanket for a pillow.

Until three Magdalena did not cry. The sixty minutes between the strokes of two and three had seemed an eternity, but hope restrained her tears. By three o'clock hope collapsed, and with it the girl's serenity. She sat down on an overturned caldron in the yard and let the tears come. Her head felt empty, and she could not, nor did she even try to, imagine what had happened to Rodrigo. All she knew was that he had not kept that decisive appointment. She let her head fall on her hands, and sat as though turned to stone. And now the minutes went rushing by as though to make up for their slow motion during the preceding hour. Magdalena was unable to move; there was no place she dared to go. She still sat, her head empty, and now without tears.

When the town-hall clock struck four, Magdalena said: "The train." And as though impelled by an invisible hand, she crossed the back yard thinking: "It's the only solution."

She stroked her bosom. "Forgive me for what I am going to do to you," she said. "But you must understand. We have no other choice. We can't live here. Who knows what might happen tomorrow? You were not for this world, my child." She lingered over the word "child." And then she went on: "Forgive me. You must forgive me. I wouldn't be able to live without you. There . . . we will be together."

She walked without knowing where she was going. A dog was baying the moon. She wanted to think about Rodrigo, but she could not. It was as though her head had been drained.

"I don't want to go to a boarding school," she said.

When she came to the railroad, she asked herself what she must do so that the train would kill her. She had often read in the newspapers that people threw themselves in front of trains, but now she did not know how to go about it. It seemed ridiculous to lie down on the track waiting for the train. She could not accept the idea.

The village clock struck the quarter-hour.

"What time will it come through?"

She began to walk down the track.

•   •   •

Renato awoke with a start. That child's crying! He clearly heard a child crying. He listened carefully. There was no doubt. But a child crying there? The nearest house was more than a kilometer away. And that crying was coming from close by. It was coming nearer.

He looked at the clock. It was quarter past four. He got up.

"Hello, there."

Magdalena looked at him in surprise, hardly recognizing him.

"Nice night, isn't it? Look at all the stars."

The girl remained silent. He hadn't even seemed surprised to see her there at that hour. He had not asked her anything. She searched Renato's face to see if she could divine his thoughts. For a moment she was afraid.

"Did they ever teach you to play with the stars?"

She did not answer.

"I'll show you. You'll see what fun it is. Sit down here."

She sat down beside him, resting her back against the wall of his house. She felt calmer.

"You can tell fortunes by looking at the stars. There's a song about it. It never comes out, but it is fun."

Magdalena began to feel better as she sat there beside this man to whom she had never spoken. He began to sing softly as he pointed to the stars:

> "*Horse of death,*
> *Horse of life,*
> *If you tell me my future,*
> *Welcome to you!*
> *Horse of death,*

Horse of life,
If you stop on Orion,
Bad luck by the bushel;
If on the Wain you stop,
Or on the Little Dipper,
Soon I will get married
To a pretty girl.
If you stop on Mars,
Mine the winning ticket,
And if on Vega, I'll die
Of a double pneumonia.
Horse of death,
Horse of life,
Where will you stop?
Where will you stop?

"Look, it stopped on Vega. That means I will die soon."
And they both laughed.

"Now let's see what it says for you."

Magdalena laughed. Renato began singing again:

"Horse of death . . .
Where will you stop?"

"At the Wain, it stopped on the Wain. What does that
mean?" asked Magdalena.

"That you will soon marry a pretty girl."

They laughed again. Just then they heard the whistle of
the oncoming train. Magdalena thought: "The train, the
train. What was I going to do with the train?"

"Wait a minute while I send the train through."

The train went by, shaking the rails, the house, and the
bench on which Magdalena was sitting.

134

After it had passed, Renato noticed that the girl's head was drooping on her shoulder.

"Are you asleep?"

She raised her head. "I'm so sleepy. . . ."

"Come," he said. "You can sleep in my house."

The headlights of the oncoming express illuminated the girl's weary face.

◇◇◇◇◇◇◇◇◇◇◇

II By noon of that September Sunday, the village pulse was not normal. Too many things had happened the day before, and Torre had not yet had time to digest them all: Don Macario's death and the rumors that circulated about his talk with Renato; the dry storm of the previous afternoon; and now the strange circumstances surrounding Magdalena's disappearance.

Doña Julia got out of bed at ten. She stretched, and called out from her room: "Magda, Magdita, it's ten o'clock."

But there was no answer. When she saw the empty, tumbled bed, she thought: "She's probably gone to early Mass. I didn't hear her." She dressed, humming Mario Costa's latest song. She threw the spread and sheets on a chair and went over to the window—and saw that the back door was open. Instinctively she put her hand in the pocket of her dressing gown. The key was not there. This surprised her very much. She went down to see if anyone had entered, and as she crossed the dining-room she saw the two drawers of the console table standing open. The silver was missing! She had been robbed. And as she was about to rush out and give the alarm, she saw a paper on the table. It said: "Good-by, Mama."

For a few moments she did not understand. Then reality hit her like a bolt of lightning. She began to tremble. Closing the drawers, she hurried to the town hall.

At exactly ten Don José Antonio appeared before the altar. He could not refrain from glancing about the church, which was emptier than ever. The mass desertion of the men had become more marked on the Sundays following the miracles. The attendance of the women had begun to fall off, and that day the parishioners hardly filled the twelve benches of the right nave.

It was a strange church, with its two naves. Apparently the plan had been to build three, but the money had run out by the time the church was half built, and they had to finish it as well as they could. The result was that it was impossible to say which was the center of the church, for the two naves were equally important.

Don José Antonio said Mass in the right nave, in a hideous, shining presbytery. And yet the young priest was proud of it. He loved cleanliness, and for that reason, when the church was being fixed up—the money had been the contribution of the miller's wife—he had thought that nothing could be better than to dignify the altar and the presbytery. For that reason he had done away with the old baroque altar of wood, having it replaced with a horrible Gothic imitation in marble. In addition, a floor and wainscoting of shiny tiles had been put in the hall of the presbytery, giving it a strange resemblance to a bathroom.

Nevertheless, Don José Antonio prided himself on his good taste. During his years in the seminary he had made an effort to keep up with the artistic movements of the day, and he had in his library the latest scandalous novelties in religious literature. But the truth is that all this was only a veneer that never really penetrated his spirit, which remained that of a peasant and conditioned all his decisions.

He had come out of the seminary with a real desire to work, and he had worked. In San Martín del Río the changes his efforts had brought about were apparent. Later he had been assigned Torre, too, and from then on he had been a priest of the road rather than of the faithful in either of the two villages, for he and his bicycle were to be seen the greater part of the time traveling the dusty road. His dream of having a motorcycle was hardly likely to come true as long as he had to skimp along on the miserable salary he received.

As he made his way to the altar, he rubbed his eyes. He had had very little sleep. He kept thinking of the letter he had in his pocket. He was worried about its possible consequences, but he knew his duty. Things such as those taking place in Torre could not be withheld from the Bishop.

"Up to now," he told himself, "Don Macario was responsible. Now I am." And during the offertory he prayed for God's help in his difficult role.

"So many Masses." He recalled Don Macario's agony. "Lord, never let me say that." And his peasant's heart, vain, perhaps, but filled with real love, rose up to the Omnipotent.

The attendance at the circle meeting was the same as at the previous ones, with the exception of Pilar, who now contemplated all this from heaven.

When Don José Antonio announced that he would be

unable to remain because he had to be in San Martín for a christening, the seven women felt a certain relief, because what they really wanted was to talk and relieve their feelings, and they were afraid Don José Antonio was going to hold forth again on a commentary of the Gospels. Only María the martyr regretted it; she always listened to the priest's words with almost supernatural respect.

Manuela led off. "Do any of you understand this business of Don Macario? Imagine, at the last hour, calling in that . . ."

María tried to smooth things out. "We don't know what he called him for. Don Macario was not a child."

"No, but he was a queer duck. And toward the end he became unbearable."

"I would have given anything to have been there. It's such a pity Marta is so deaf and didn't hear anything."

"And then the bells . . ."

"That's witchcraft. Can you imagine God up and ringing the bells when that's what the sacristan is for? If he had cured Don Macario or something like that, but . . ."

"Or let that storm yesterday bring rain."

"Or converted all the atheists in this village."

"Yes, converted . . ." She was on the point of saying "Sátrapa," but caught herself. ". . . all the atheists in the village."

"And to think that at first we believed . . ."

"At first?" María parried. "He hasn't done anything bad for us not to believe in him."

The miller's widow bristled. "Nothing bad? What about the drought?"

"That's not his fault."

"But he could have remedied it. All he had to do was ask for it."

138

"What do we know?"

"There was a silence. "It would have been so nice," the blue twin said.

"What would have been so nice?"

"Suppose he had worked a lot of miracles, and people had come here from many villages, and trains, and cars . . . and . . ."

"And it had been like Lourdes."

On this point the miller's widow was an authority. She had been at Lourdes and boasted about it as if the French village was her child. She had already told a thousand times about everything she had seen there, plus the new details she added with every telling. This time all she said was: "Like Lourdes."

And she tried to picture the French basilica beside the lake and the village full of little shops selling rosaries and medals. As though her thought had gone leaping from mind to mind, all of them recalled what they had seen in pictures that she had brought back with her, the collection that opened up like an accordion.

It was then that Lucio called out from the door: "Have you heard the news?" And he proceeded to tell them about Magdalena's disappearance and Doña Julia's state, drowning in her own tears.

"It serves her right for being so stupid. Everybody in town knew about it except her."

"Knew about what?"

"That the girl and Rodrigo were seeing each other. I'd be willing to swear . . ."

"No," María shouted. "That angel!"

"Just come down from heaven! Why, they were kissing every chance they got."

"But she was so good."

"What in the devil do you call good? What more did you want her to do?"

María tried to answer, but she did not know what to say.

"And what about her mother, another piece off the same bolt? Does she think we don't know about her carrying on with the druggist?"

"Look." The blue twin ran to the window. "There they go." Several more windows opened.

Doña Julia, escorted by the mayor and the druggist, was on her way to the station. Nobody there knew anything about the girl. "You can be sure she did not take the train here. Unless she went to Marzales to get the five-o'clock . . ."

"What if she went to . . ."

"Nobody takes the silver to go and commit suicide."

"If she went to Marzales to get the five-o'clock, maybe the switchman saw her. He's usually up by four."

"I can't get to sleep," Magdalena had said.

"You just try. Go on."

Renato was sitting in a corner of the room under a window covered with burlap. The girl was lying across from him, in his bed. She kept turning and twisting.

"I'm sorry I haven't got a better bed for you."

"It's not the bed."

There was a silence. Then the girl suddenly said: "You know I was going to commit suicide?"

"Yes. Don't talk about that now."

"I was in mortal sin."

"Who can say?"

Magdalena sat up in bed, her eyes gleaming. "Tell me that I would have been saved!"

Renato shook his head and smiled. "How do you expect me to know?"

Magdalena buried her head in the pillow, sobbing.

"Now, stop tormenting yourself. We know so little. Let Him punish you, but let Him understand, too. . . ."

"But, you know, I am expecting a baby. And I wanted to commit suicide. . . ." She said this with the naturalness with which she might have confessed some childish prank. Then her voice broke. "It would have been much better to die. Why didn't you let me . . . end it?"

Renato sat with his head buried in his hands. The first light of day was coming through the window. "That would have been the worst thing. A sin of pride."

"I only wanted to protect my child."

"You're protecting him now. With those tears."

Tears were running slowly down her cheeks, a timid and humble weeping. "Tell me that you, at least, don't think badly of me."

"What a child you are!" He laughed and, going over to her, stroked her braids.

"I'm so tired."

"There now, lie down, and try to go to sleep." He covered her gently, and stood looking at her.

In a barely audible voice she said: "I'm afraid."

"Don't worry. I will be with you."

Doña Julia let out a screech when she saw on the switchman's bench the package clearly revealing the shape of the silverware. And when she raised her hand to rap at the door, it opened.

"Yes, she's here." And then: "Be quiet, she's asleep."

1 4 1

The tavern that morning was as crowded as on holidays. El Moro dragged his wooden leg from one end of the counter to the other, unable to handle all the orders. Uncle Lucas was pontificating in his corner. The storm the other afternoon . . . Who would have thought it was going to be nothing more than a few claps of thunder? Renato's name came up repeatedly in the conversations, and each time it left a bad taste. The tide of hate was rising. All the curses held back, and even the spoken ones, were piling up in every heart. Something had to give or they would die of suffocation. But what good did it do to despair? If it was a question of leveling a mountain, they would find the strength somehow. But bringing the rain was not leveling a mountain. Get rid of Renato? If that would do any good . . .

Sátrapa came in, and all eyes turned to him. El Moro hurried to serve him. Sátrapa downed a double cognac.

Someone laid a hand on his shoulder. "We were talking about Renato. What do you think?"

The village magnate fashioned an ironic smile: "All this is going to wind up badly."

And a smile went around the tavern.

Steam was rising from Manuela's stove as a hand rapped on the window. It was Carmela.

"Have you heard? What a scandal!"

"Who would ever have thought . . ."

"This is the limit. People are known by the company they keep."

"To take that slut in . . ."

"Whatever is the world coming to!"

"This is all the devil's doing. And they say she is going to live with him."

"The pig!"

"And Doña Julia says she never wants to see her again."

"Naturally, if a daughter of mine . . ."

From the dining-room Lucio shouted: "Is that soup coming or isn't it?"

Manuela slammed the window shut. "Heavens, what a humor you're in!" And she carried in the steaming soup.

"Who was it?"

"Carmela."

"What was on her mind?"

"Renato. I said it from the first day: this is the devil's work, and nothing else. And to think the miller's widow was saying that this could have been like Lourdes."

Lucio stared at her. "Did she say that?"

"She certainly did. And that tourists and sick people would come from all over Spain."

Lucio laughed. "You know, that's not such a bad idea. We could . . ."

"But it's the devil's doing."

After a thoughtful pause, Lucio answered: "Let there be miracles even if the devil works them."

Manuela could not understand why her husband smiled.

It was midafternoon when Sátrapa went walking about the deserted threshing-floors. The sun's rays bore straight down, an autumn sun but still strong. The magnate walked steadily, his handkerchief protecting his baldness. He tried to think of Matilde, but he found no pleasure in the thought. With that suffocating air. When he reached his floor, he sat down on a slate bench beside the shed in which the implements were kept. The other floors were deserted, and Sátrapa sat there looking at his idle threshing machine. He lost all notion of time.

"Hot, isn't it?"

Before him stood a young fellow he did not recognize. Sátrapa was annoyed because he had been unable to repress a start on hearing the greeting. He looked at the lad. He was wearing gray pants and a corduroy jacket. His hair was reddish, and several locks fell over his forehead. Every now and then he shook them back, but in a few minutes they had fallen over his forehead again. The lad sat down beside him without saying a word. Sátrapa was surprised by this familiarity, all the more because he did not know him. "He must not be from the village."

"A bad year, isn't it?" the stranger remarked.

"It certainly is," Sátrapa answered.

"And it's all the fault of that . . ."

Sátrapa looked the lad in the eye. They were extraordinarily bright eyes that were never quiet. How did he know that if . . . "Are you from the village?"

"No."

"I thought so."

There was a pause, and then the young fellow said: "What I can't figure out is how you put up with him."

"What in the devil do you want us to do?"

The lad's smile broadened. "Get rid of him. And that's the end of it."

"Get rid of him? As if that took care of anything . . ."

"Who knows! It might take care of everything." Another pause. Then he went on: "Where I come from he wouldn't have lasted a month."

"And where do you come from?"

"Oh, a long way from here. No, it's not hard to liquidate a person."

"But risky."

"Risky if you do it in public. But suppose a man is

found dead on the road. Everybody hated him. There's no way of knowing who killed him. It might have been anybody. The judge may be troublesome at first. Then he gets nervous. The papers pile up. Finally the judge forgets about it."

"Oh, sure. Talk is cheap."

Just then a girl came running toward them from the other edge of the threshing-fields. The young man said: "There comes your daughter."

Sátrapa recognized María Belén's limp. The child was sweating.

"Mother fell out of the attic. She's dying. Come quick."

For a second Sátrapa did not move. Then without a word he began to run. Halfway home he asked himself how the stranger had known that the girl was his daughter. He turned his head and saw that she was limping after him as fast as she could, but he did not see the young man. Sátrapa shrugged his shoulders and quickened his pace. His belly swung as he ran.

María Belén could run no more and she sat down on a stone. Then she began to walk toward her house. Suddenly, and without knowing why, she changed direction and set out for Renato's house.

12

It was striking seven as Renato reached the threshold of Sátrapa's house. He stopped and ran his coat sleeve over his forehead. Then he realized that someone had been running after him. It was Matilde. Renato looked her up and down, and anyone watching him would have seen in that glance the greatest compassion and the greatest severity. But even the compassion was cold, for it knew itself to be useless.

Matilde grabbed him by the arm. "Where are you going?"

Renato stood disconcerted, for he did not really know where he was going. María Belén had told him that her mother was dying, and he had set out at a run without even thinking where he was going.

The woman went on: "What are you going to do?"

This was something else that Renato had not asked himself. What was he going to do? Or, rather, was he going to do anything? He felt somewhat ashamed of the pell-mell run he had made without stopping to think for one second. He felt like a gun whose trigger someone had pulled and which had no choice but to fire. But he was not going to start thinking there at the door. He pulled his arm loose. "Leave me alone."

She let go. She felt defeated in her first attempt. Her tone of voice changed completely, and she ventured only to say imploringly: "Don't do that."

Halfway up the stairs, Renato turned his head with an impulse to ask her what it was that he should not do, but he went on up.

Matilde stood crying beside the wall. Once more life was eluding her. César had said to her half an hour before: "We'll get married. My wife is dying."

She had not known whether to laugh or not.

He had laughed. "Don Melquíades has said we have to get her to the capital at once or else she's a goner. Her ribs are buried in her lungs and she's suffocating."

"So what did you do?"

"I called an ambulance . . . for tomorrow."

María was flickering out minute by minute, like a lamp whose supply of oil is gone. That whistle from her wounded lungs was growing fainter with each breath.

Sátrapa opened the window from time to time to see if the ambulance he knew would not arrive was coming.

It would have been about quarter of seven when Don Melquíades laid his hand on Sátrapa's shoulder. "This is nearly over."

Five minutes later Sátrapa was doing his best to squeeze out a tear.

Renato's dark face looked more tense and gloomy than ever as he appeared in the doorway. "Go out," he ordered.

Nobody even tried to protest. Various heads were lowered and almost knocked together trying to get out of the door, as though fearful that some misfortune was about to take place in that room. There came the sound of a closing door.

Renato stood with his hands clasped on the bars at the foot of the bed. María's head—serene—rested on the pillow, and only the handkerchief tied under her chin to hold her lower jaw in place lent the scene a tragic air. Renato stood motionless. What had he come here to do?

He moved closer to the bed and untied the knot that held the handkerchief. The mouth fell open with the sound of a split apple.

It had grown dark very quickly, and he turned on the light. And at the very moment that the bulb began to glow he noted a tremor in the body of the dead woman. Renato spoke: "You could get up."

Almost ten minutes elapsed between the first movement of María's head and the complete return of life. Her cheeks took on color, and now she had the air of a woman who was sleeping.

Renato laid his hand on her shoulder and shook her gently. "Come on."

She opened her eyes almost normally, as though awakening from a short nap. She breathed quietly. She turned her head to the left, as though she wanted to go back to sleep, and pressed the pillow against her face. Then, as though frightened, she suddenly raised her head. She looked slowly around the room. She fixed her eyes on Renato as though she did not recognize him, sat up slowly without saying a single word, and looked again at Renato, who was watching her, in silence, too, from the foot of the bed.

She did all this with the air of a sleepwalker. Then suddenly she covered her face with her hands and began to cry.

Renato watched her without knowing what to do. He wished to console her, but he did not know for what. The situation seemed to him ridiculous, and he could imagine the people pressed against the door, listening to that crying

148

and not venturing to come in. He ran his hand over his forehead, and it came away damp. He even asked himself if he was not dreaming. He felt somewhat as he had felt on the day of the cross. Now, as then, he felt empty.

María finally spoke. "It was a mistake."

Renato asked himself: "A mistake? What was a mistake?" And he could not discover in what he had been mistaken.

She shook her head and said, still crying: "You did wrong. I was happy. For always." She looked at him deeply. "You don't know what it means to be happy for always. Not to suffer, of course, but much more than that."

The silence now became more tense. There were tears in María's eyes.

"And now to come back here, to wait for him. Hours, hours, knowing that he is with . . . her." The tears rolled down her cheeks. "Now it is going to be much harder. . . ."

She paused a moment to smooth back her hair. Then she spoke in a still deeper tone. "I regret it most of all for God. If I were dead, they could get married and they would sin no more. Now . . ."

Renato ran his hand over his forehead again, and once more asked himself if he was not dreaming.

She said softly: "Now, you see, you've spoiled everything."

Renato felt a need to run, to flee, but he barely had the strength to raise his head and see that the door was open—when, who had opened it?—and that the stairway was filled with people. In the front rank he saw Sátrapa, in whose eyes such hatred had settled as he could never have believed a man could encompass. And he was afraid.

149

But when Renato made his way to the stairs, the group opened up as though a spring had been pressed, and he passed in silence through the two silent rows of villagers.

The mayor's wife said: "You shouldn't have got mixed up in these things, Sebastián. If it's Fatso's business, let him handle it."

"But I am the mayor," Don Sebastián protested.

"The mayor! A lot of mayoring you do!"

Don Sebastián cleared his throat as he nervously polished his glasses.

His wife said: "For two nights I have dreamed about Renato."

He looked at her in bewilderment. Then he shrugged his shoulders, without understanding.

Sátrapa spoke at the meeting in the town hall. "I think the time has come to take this business seriously. We must . . ." But not even he dared to complete the phrase. There was a long silence.

"Winter is coming on," Uncle Lucas said.

"The thought is frightening," Don Melquíades added.

Sátrapa was scowling. He would have liked somebody else to propose what he was thinking and was afraid to propose.

Lucio moved restlessly in his chair in his eagerness to expound his great idea. "It has occurred to me," and he paused a moment to heighten the effect, "that the miracles could be exploited."

"Exploited?"

"Yes, exploited. Tourists would come and leave money in the village."

A spark began to glow in Sátrapa's eyes.

"We could make candles, crosses, souvenirs," Lucio went on.

At this point Sátrapa broke into a coarse guffaw that grew louder and louder. He got up, choking with laughter, and slapped the frail back of Lucio, the sacristan.

◇◇◇◇◇◇◇◇◇◇◇

13   Irola now has a population of twelve thousand. It has had as many as seventeen thousand inhabitants, but this is not its period of prosperity. It is one of the many cities that have at one time made history and today live on the memory of those happier days, bypassed by industries that established themselves in more prosperous regions. Today Irola is a city of cautious coupon-clippers who grow poorer and more cautious every day. The institutions that in other days gave luster to the city—schools, distinguished families, the chapterhouses of certain religious orders—have all departed the place, which soon will be nothing but a big village. Today only two glories remain to it: being head of the diocese and capital of the province, and there is even talk that both honors will be transferred to more flourishing cities.

Nevertheless, Irola has two newspapers, which appear on alternate days. On Mondays, Wednesdays, and Fridays *The Voice of Irola* comes out, and on Tuesdays, Thursdays, and Saturdays *The Light of Irola* serves up its sauce of news. As both papers come out in late-afternoon editions, both editors rest on Sundays and can spend one whole day running each other down. Despite the cordial dislike the editors profess for each other, the contents of the two papers are practically identical. Perhaps the only difference is that in *The Voice* it is Don José Miguel Caballo Blanco—an illustrious son of Irola who now holds the chair of art at the University of Madrid—who publishes dry-as-dust articles on the history of Irola, whereas the signer of the dry-as-dust articles on the history of Irola published in *The Light* is Don Luis Tomás Toro Delgado—a no less illustrious native son who occupies a similar chair at the University of Barcelona.

If Don César telephoned *The Voice*, it was not, God knows, because he had any preference for either of the newspapers—on the contrary, he took them both with exemplary impartiality—but simply because "the affair of his wife" took place on a Sunday and *The Voice* would come out the next day. And so it happened, thanks to this insignificant chance, that Don Cayetano instead of Don Tadeo chalked up one of the most important scoops of the year.

That September 9 had been a completely routine day for Don Cayetano. Like the solid citizen and lukewarm Christian he was, he had gone to twelve-o'clock Mass; he had had his *apéritif*—beer and shrimps—at the Casa Dorada; he had eaten the usual Sunday *paella*, and had played a game of dominoes to see who paid for coffee. He had lost. Afterwards he had taken his customary walk with Doña Sofía. And while waiting for dinner he had gone over to the newspaper office to start work on the next day's edition.

The editorial office of *The Voice* is not a beehive of activity; as a matter of fact, Don Cayetano comprises its whole staff. It is in a room about fifteen feet square, divided by a dust-darkened glass partition, with two windows marked "Advertisements" and "Subscriptions." To tell the truth, Don Cayetano and a good pair of shears were all that was needed to put out *The Voice*. With half a dozen clippings from the Madrid papers, the articles Don José Miguel sent in each week, a few advertisements of old moving pictures, cattle feed, and seeds, and, as a special feature, the names of the performers of an occasional circus that came through Irola by mistake, the paper was made up. At times his oldest son, José Carlos, contributed reports signed "Special Service," but not too often. Don Cayetano did not favor excesses of any sort.

As for the windows, very rarely were the two in operation at the same time, and whether you went to leave an advertisement or a subscription, you invariably found Don Cayetano smiling behind his glasses and with a cigarette stub—perhaps it was always the same one—hanging from the corner of his mouth. Don Cayetano had given seven hostages to fortune. Most of them were still small, and he could not "indulge himself in superfluities."

Nor could the décor of the office have been simpler. On the right wall hung a huge map of Spain fastened with eight thumbtacks. On the opposite one, a large painting of a battle scene. It might have been any one, but at the bottom an inscription read "Waterloo." The only noteworthy feature was a border of wall around the picture which was so much cleaner than the rest that it could only mean that at some time a larger picture had hung there. And so it had. First it had been a handsome photograph of the wedding of Alfonso XIII. This was followed by one of Primo de Rivera. When the Republic came, Don Cayetano, tired of so many changes, settled on the battle of Waterloo, which was safer and not affected by the veering winds of politics. Because Don Cayetano—and the same held true of all Irola—had little interest in politics. So long as *The Voice* could go on filling the seven mouths of his seven offspring, one system was as good as another as far as he was concerned. Not Communism; no, not that. He did not have too clear an idea of what it was, but he identified it with the rule of the unwashed. The sentiments of all the inhabitants of Irola were pretty much the same, except, of course, for the unwashed of the poor quarters.

When the telephone rang that night, Don Cayetano was not thinking about political problems or the definition of Communism, but about the scissors he had been trying to find in the pile of newspaper clippings. He reached out lazily for the receiver, prepared to jot down the name of some new fertilizer, and said in a bored voice: "Hello."

But when the voice of Don César came over the wire, telling him some weird story about miracles, he sat up in his chair, snubbed out his cigarette butt in the ash tray, and said eagerly: "Yes, yes, go ahead."

Don Cayetano no longer needed to look for the missing scissors. He even allowed himself the luxury of stuffing into an envelope all the clippings that had piled up on the table. It was not often that a story like this came his way. Don Cayetano felt himself one of God's anointed, proud of the service he was rendering Him by giving publicity to a miracle of this sort. And would this wipe Don Tadeo's eye!

Illustrious and Reverend Sir: This morning I posted a letter to Your Excellency setting forth the happenings that have so stirred Torre de Muza during these recent months. If I am writing you again, it is because in the last few hours two other incidents have taken place which bear on the case under our consideration. I shall endeavor to set them before Your Excellency with all possible brevity.

. . . .

Your Excellency can imagine the comments to which this first incident has given rise. The fact that Renato should take under his protection a girl publicly recognized as "fallen" has made a deplorable impression on the upright members of the community, and, in my opinion, it was, at the very least, a most imprudent act.

Another piece of information bearing on this same point concerns the strange words of the switchman to certain of the aforesaid pious members of the community. (Though I am in duty bound to inform Your Excellency that I was not an actual witness, and it may be that when they were repeated to me their content was altered.)

Apparently, when the mother of the girl in question refused to let her come home, the switchman said the girl would stay and live with him, a thing that shocked the village deeply, inasmuch as Renato lives absolutely alone.

Some of the women who are most helpful to me in my apostolic duties did their best to prevent this, and pleaded with the girl's mother to take her back, but in vain. They then went to the switchman's house, who at first refused to receive them, but afterward told them to take her into their homes, and finally he turned on them and insulted them (so they tell me). The ladies in question thought—and, in my opinion, rightly—that to receive her would be to condone what she had done, and that they should not do it unless the girl publicly requested forgiveness. Whereupon Renato, "as excited as a madman," so they told me, said that they were the ones who were not fit to receive her and that the girl "would become contaminated in the foul air of those homes without God." I can certify the irreproachableness of these people. Though I should add that I think their intervention in the matter was tactless, inasmuch as Renato's morality is above question, or so it seemed when all these matters began. (On this point there is no change from what I informed Your Excellency of in my letter this morning.)

But the interest in all this was completely overshadowed by what happened this afternoon. It was about seven o'clock when . . .

Your Excellency can well understand the effect that an event of this nature has had in a village like this. Even I find myself completely at sea. I have not had time to make a thoroughgoing study of the problem, which I feel falls within the province of persons of greater competence than mine. The moment has come, I feel, for the direct intervention of the ecclesiastical authorities.

The village, for the most part, has taken no stand in the matter. There are those who are inclined to see it as a true intervention of God, though they refrain from saying this openly because of the strange incidents connected with what happened this afternoon.

However, there are many more who see in it the intervention of the devil, and for that reason they are afraid to discuss it, and I have even observed that there are those who cross themselves when the name of Renato is spoken.

It has seemed to me that Your Excellency might be interested in knowing—though this does not in any way affect the need for deeper study—the opinion of the two *persons most directly concerned in the matter: María and the doctor.*

I have asked the doctor for a written report, which I am including with this letter. You will see from it that Don Melquíades has his reservations, due, perhaps, to fear of undermining his professional reputation, or to a reluctance to become involved in a dubious and notorious incident. It is my impression that he is confused and bewildered. He keeps repeating that he has never seen anything of the sort, but the word "God" never once crosses his lips.

As for María, she does not know how to write, so I limited myself to questioning her, and I have endeavored to set down the results for you as faithfully as I can. I want to tell you beforehand that she is an exceptional woman, and if we mortals were in a position to judge by what we see, I would not hesitate to classify her as the person closest to God in all Torre de Muza.

She seemed stunned by what had happened, and especially by the avalanche of questions of her neighbors. When I went to see her she sat down across the table from me as though she were on the witness stand, and I had to extract the answers from her as with a forceps. This is a fairly accurate transcript of our talk:

"Have you a clear awareness of the fact of dying?"

"Yes."

"You don't have the least doubt?"

"None."

"What did you feel?"

"That I had died."

"What else?"

"Nothing else."

"*Yes, but what was dying like?*"

"*I don't know. To be finished, to die.*" She made vague gestures as she said this without being able to express herself.

"*And after death, did you have a clear awareness of being in the other life?*"

"*I don't know. I think so.*"

"*What was it like?*"

"*Lots of light.*"

"*Light? Light how?*"

"*I don't know. Light.*"

"*But did you feel yourself alive in the other life?*"

"*Yes, certainly.*"

"*Did you feel yourself alive like now?*"

"*No, it was different.*"

"*Do you recall if you were judged?*"

"*I don't know. I don't think so.*"

"*No?*"

"*I don't think so.*"

"*Theology says that the Judgment comes immediately after death.*"

"*I don't know about that. It was like . . .*"

"*Like what?*"

"*. . . like if a hand . . .*"

"*A hand?*"

"*. . . took hold of you.*"

"*Then you did not feel completely dead?*"

"*Yes, dead, yes.*"

"*Free, then. As if you were not completely free there, as if you were not completely alive . . .*"

"*Maybe it was that.*"

"*Do you have the sense of having been in heaven?*"

158

"*No, I don't think so.*"

"*Or in hell?*"

"*No!*"

"*Or in purgatory?*"

"*I don't think so. In another place.*"

"*In another place?*"

"*I don't know. I think so.*"

"*Did you see God?*"

"*Yes, that is something you can't forget.*"

"*What was it like?*"

At this point it took her a long time to answer. As though she were unable to put anything so great into words. Finally she said: "Happy."

"*Happy?*"

"*Yes, happy.*" *As she said this, her face lighted up as though she did not know were she was. She seemed truly happy, but with a special kind of happiness.*

"*And then when you came back to life, what was it like?*"

"*Sad.*"

"*Sad?*"

"*Yes, like being dragged, like . . .*"

"*. . . like?*"

"*. . . like being pulled back. Taken away from the light.*"

"*How did the light go away?*"

"*It went away.*"

"*Where did it go?*"

"*I don't know. It went away.*"

"*And when you came back to life?*"

"*Sadness. A great sadness.*"

"*And your body?*"

"Numb. Like after a beating."

"Did you feel a pain in your back where the wound was before?"

"No, I didn't feel any pain; just . . ."

"Just what?"

"Tired."

She said all this with her eyes almost closed. She really gave the impression of being very tired.

"Do you believe there was a true intervention of God?"

She raised her head quickly. "Of course."

"You are not afraid that it may be a snare of the dev—?"

"No!" She cut me short without letting me finish the word. It was the only quick answer she gave during our entire talk.

"Why are you so sure?"

"I am calm."

"And why?"

"I feel a great peace."

"And why?"

"God is happy."

Her eyes gleamed with an extraordinary brightness, but they clearly revealed how hard it was for her to talk about the matter, how much she was in need of rest. For that reason I let her go, in the hope that, if you so decide, the ecclesiastical authorities can question her in more detail.

It is now midnight, Your Excellency, and I, too, find myself extremely tired. I have decided to spend the night in Torre, in Don Macario's old house, in the event of further happenings that might easily lead to violence. The first reaction this evening was fear, but later I noticed

hate in many eyes, and I have even heard that there is talk
of setting fire to Renato's house so he will have to leave
the village. The people are panic-stricken, and they would
feel relieved if Renato went away. I think it is worth con-
sidering this solution. At least his temporary removal—
taking him to a monastery in the capital or elsewhere—
might be a wise move so the village would calm down.
But, of course, that is a matter for Your Excellency to
decide.

And that is all for today. I shall keep Your Excellency
informed of everything that happens.

Your most devoted son respectfully kisses your pasto-
ral ring.

Renato shifted position on the cement bench. He
moved his face and it hurt. He was utterly exhausted. He
rested his head on his left arm. "Why?" The night was
frighteningly clear. A huge moon lighted up the plain
and bathed all the village in a gentle milky light. Renato
sat up straighter and arched his back, which hurt as
though he had received a beating. He felt as though his
body were not his, as though it hung on him like a sack. It
seemed to him, too, that he had a false forehead, as
though another had been slipped over his own. "Why do
these things have to happen to me?" He recalled that
when he came away from Sátrapa's house he had had to
cling to the gate to keep from falling. Suddenly he had
the feeling that he had committed a crime, that he had
deprived someone of life. Perhaps this was why he felt a
need to run, to flee from something, without knowing
what. Now he was exhausted.

"I'll never come back again," he thought. "Never, never
again." Yes, it was dangerous to come back. God was

playing too hard a game with him. Now everything was becoming dangerous, to walk, to talk, to move. "I am God's glove, nothing more." And he repeated many times: "A glove, a glove, a glove." Why did he suddenly feel conquered by that inexorable hand which led him to work the strangest miracles? He trembled as the word "miracle" came into his mind. "But you have to be a saint to do them," he shouted. His words echoed with a stupid sound in the silence. He sat up. "I am going crazy." He looked at the sky. "You've got no right, You understand. You've got no right." He clenched his teeth as he spoke. Then he felt the tears rising in his eyes. "Or maybe You do. . . ." He shook his head slowly. "It used to be so easy to be happy. This happiness now is beautiful, but . . . so hard."

He tried to get up, but he could not stand straight. He dropped back onto the bench, which encircled the hermitage of Our Lady of the Dark Eyes. He had sought refuge there because he did not venture to go back to his house. "Poor María!" he said. "Truly I have deprived her of life. This is a real crime." He asked himself why he had done it, why he had run there like mad when he had heard the news. "Perhaps she is not completely dead and I will just revive her." He felt happy as he thought this. "Yes, that must have been it. How could it be possible that . . . ?"

The village lay sleeping at his feet like a tired animal. "Why don't You take mercy on them once and for all? Show Yourself to them, let them see You. Maybe that would be enough. What can they know? They have fashioned themselves a little God. A plumber God." He laughed as he heard himself say this. He repeated it: "A plumber God, that is what they have made of You. They only call on you when there is something to be fixed. When the faucets of heaven don't work." He laughed again. "But what in the devil do You expect them to understand?"

◇◇◇◇◇◇◇◇◇◇

14 Monday morning the mayor of Irola said to his wife: "Say, do you remember if it was in Torre de Muza that the business about a cross that fell in the lake happened? Well, today there's been a better miracle there."

The Bishop of Irola said: "God help us, this is a complicated affair."

The editor of *El Día* of Madrid said: "This sounds like news. We'd better get Ponce there."

Ponce said: "Thank God. At least it will be a change. I'm fed up with Grace Kelly's wedding."

Sátrapa said: "Well, let's hope that we get some fun out of it."

María the martyr said: "May God bring us safely through all this."

María Belén said: "Will they build a shrine, Mama?"

Uncle Lucas said: "I almost regret it. This year's loans would have been good business."

The prior of the Augustine order in Irola said to the lay brother: "Get one of the guest rooms ready. The Bishop is sending us this miracle fellow from Torre."

The lay brother thought: "I thank Thee, Lord, for this privilege of seeing a saint."

An old canon of Irola said: "Couldn't these good people leave God in peace?"

A young canon of Irola thought: "How I would like to be appointed to the investigation committee." It seemed to him a lack of humility to add that it would be fitting in view of his profound theological attainments.

The old woman said: "Dear God! Dear God!"

Matilde said: "The martyr must be happy today with her name in all the newspapers!"

Lucio said: "It was a wonderful idea, wonderful. The church will be full and the collection boxes . . ."

Manuela said: "You will be the sacristan of a basilica, of a big basilica."

Carmen said: "Who would have thought that God was going to make of this something that would be to His glory?"

Carmela said: "What if it should be the devil's doing?"

The miller's widow said: "The devil wouldn't do anything to glorify God. This is going to be another Lourdes. Just wait and see how wonderful the pilgrimages will be!"

Don José Antonio said: "Those damned journalists have got wind of this. Who in the devil put them on the scent?"

María Belén asked: "And will they make a statue of Renato, Mama?"

By noon the mayor of Irola was thinking: "You know, this business of the miracles might attract tourists and would help my farm exhibit."

El Moro said: "We'll have to fix up this tavern. And if it weren't . . . I'd even set up a crucifix. In the end I will."

Father Mendizábal said: "Is it possible that in that village where not one man wanted to go to confession . . . ?"

The old woman said: "Dear God! Dear God!"

Lena de Castro said: "Papa, you have to take me to Torre de Muza. It must be wonderful. And I'll wear my new suit."

Perote called out: "*The Voooice of Irooola*. Read all about the miracle."

In the Casino, Don Jorge held forth: "We will never emerge from the Middle Ages."

Don Tadeo said: "God might work miracles on Mondays, Wednesdays, or Fridays! It looks like Don Cayetano has a deal with the Almighty. I'm just as good a Christian as he is."

Doña Serafina, with a telegram in her hands, said to Don Cayetano in a voice trembling with emotion: "Look, my dear, *El Tiempo* of Madrid wants you to act as their special correspondent. Praise God for His blessings on this house."

Fede said: "Taxi to Torre de Muza? Three hundred and fifty pesetas, a special price for you."

La Tarde bannered its final edition: "Unprecedented Miracle in a Village of Castile."

The next morning the headlines of the *Correo de España* read: "Woman Raised from the Dead Gives Her Impressions of What She Saw in the Other World. The Most Sensational News Coverage."

The headlines of *La Voz de la Iglesia* ran: "The Church Has Not Yet Passed Judgment on the Miracles of Torre de Muza."

Renato, looking up with a smile on his lips, said: "Thanks for not playing any tricks on me today."

◇◇◇◇◇◇◇◇◇◇

15 Don Jerónimo Ferrara had been mayor of Irola for four years. An ambitious man if ever there was one, he would stoop to anything he could profit by. In the Jesuit school as a boy he had been a typical informer, the hanger-on of the prefects, always ready to run with the hare and hunt with the hounds. The nickname "Brown-nose," which had been conferred on him in his second year of preparatory school, suited him to a tee.

His life had always been utterly commonplace. Brown-nose would never reach the top on his own merits, but he was smart enough to know it. And so he devoted his best energies to sizing up those of his associates who might make the grade, and cultivating them. In this way he had won the good will of Don Angel Salvadores, a former professor of his at the University of Salamanca, and for the past four years Minister of the Interior, exactly the four years of Don Jerónimo's incumbence in Irola. To be sure, the post was one of the worst in the country, but it was a matter of only a few years, and if he did something that attracted attention it might lead to a better-paying appointment.

In Irola, employing the methods that had won him his nickname, he had captured the good opinion of the solid citizenry from the first moment, from that very six o'clock in the afternoon of that Maundy Thursday when he had assumed the mayoralty.

The outgoing mayor of Irola still remembered it as the worst moment of his life. This was what had happened. The new mayor reached the city at five in the afternoon. After the regulation speeches came the sumptuous collation that had been prepared at the Hotel Canciller. The room was crowded with the cream of Irola, and the waiters moved busily about, carrying trays of glasses, sandwiches, and canapés, waiting for the mayor to start the party going. All the guests whiled away the wait, clearing their throats and studying the contents of each tray.

When Luis, the waiter with the brightest smile and the choicest tray, went over to the new mayor, the latter made a slight gesture of embarrassment.

"Oh," he said, "you will have to forgive me, but on Maundy Thursday and Good Friday I fast. I take only bread and water."

It took the organizers of the festivity a few seconds

to react. It would hardly be the thing for the guests to stuff themselves with canapés and sandwiches while the leading authority took nothing but a piece of bread and a glass of water—bread and water, moreover, that were not easy to lay hands on at that moment. Coughs and approving smiles were exchanged while people looked at one another without knowing how to break the ice.

At this point one of the aldermen spoke up: "We might go and visit the monuments."

The mayor of Irola turned as though somebody had stepped on his corn, thinking that Don Jerónimo was going to detect the irony that underlay the words. But Don Jerónimo beamed: "That is a fine idea."

The mayor swallowed hard. He tried to smile. "Yes, yes indeed, that would be very pleasant. And, besides, the cathedral is . . . yes, the cathedral is very . . . pleasant."

Nobody noticed how the waiters disappeared.

This gesture of the new mayor was widely commented on in Irola, and Don Jerónimo soon found himself very popular. At the Casino they began to call him Saint Jerónimo, and in many houses they made fun of him. But at bottom they all admired him, for to the Irolans fasting on bread and water was a mark of sanctity such as they had never thought was really carried out. Don Jerónimo, moreover, took good care to keep up this reputation, and it was soon known that his confessor was Father Bosch, the best orator in the city, and every Sunday he could be seen devoutly taking communion in the Church of the Redemptorists.

What was worrying Don Jerónimo now was the matter of his promotion. He had thought that the post in Irola would be a matter of a couple of years; four long years

168

had gone by, and he was still stuck in this dull province. He felt that he must do something to remind the people in Madrid that he was still waiting. But it was not easy to find the needed opportunity in Irola. Finally Don Jerónimo hit upon the idea of an agricultural exhibit. But as the opening day drew near, the mayor began to fret about who would come to his exhibit. He knew that he could count on the support of the Irolans, who attended en masse the laying of the cornerstone of every new building. But this public was not enough to make Madrid sit up and take notice of the exhibit.

Tourists, that was what he needed, tourists. And the truth of the matter was that nobody who did not have business in Irola ever came through except by mistake. For Irola, besides suffering from poor communications, had nothing to attract the interest of tourists. Its artistic treasure was limited to walls that had more patches than a nun's habit; a cathedral, half Gothic, half baroque —that is to say, neither Gothic nor baroque; a town hall of the seventeenth century on whose main balcony Isabel II had once appeared; and two utterly commonplace statues of two illustrious Irolans of whom nobody had ever heard outside of Irola: Castellanos, a long-dead bishop, and General Aguilas. With such elements, Don Jerónimo realized that there was no basis for tourist propaganda. To make matters worse, the thermometer dropped below zero in winter, and in summer rose above ninety.

This being the case, it is easy to understand the satisfaction with which Don Jerónimo viewed the idea of the miracles of Torre.

It would have been around four in the afternoon when he heard the quavering voice of Don Sebastián over the wire.

"Oh, yes, I have already read this morning's report in the newspaper."

". . . . ."

"No, no, don't you worry. On the contrary, I am really pleased that all this has happened."

". . . . ."

"Order, naturally; order must be maintained, but it must not stand in the way of events, not at all. We cannot forget that Spain is a Catholic country."

". . . . ."

"Yes, and even back them up. I can see nothing wrong in that."

". . . . ."

"But don't you have a railroad?"

". . . . ."

"Well, then, all you have to do is ask for a special train."

". . . . ."

"Naturally, of course, I understand."

". . . . ."

"But that's no problem. You can send that man away for a while."

". . . . ."

"That's right; why don't you bring him here to me?"

". . . . ."

"Oh, that's no problem. We'll decide here what to do. We could even turn him over to the Bishop."

". . . . ."

"Why not this very afternoon? What do you think?"

". . . . ."

"I'll send my car."

". . . . ."

"No trouble at all. It's a pleasure."

". . . . ."

"Good. Then I'll tell my chauffeur to call for you, and I'll expect you around seven."

". . . . ."

"Fine."

". . . . ."

"That'll be fine."

". . . . ."

"I'll be seeing you soon."

Don Jerónimo stroked his mustache. He was really pleased with himself. Besides, he realized that he felt a certain curiosity to see this man who raised crosses and the dead. Real curiosity.

Don Sebastián hung up the receiver, took a long breath, and dropped back in his chair.

Sátrapa was radiant as he got up and poured out a glass of cognac. "Sebastián, you couldn't have handled it better."

The mayor of Torre was pale. Sátrapa laid a hand on his shoulder and gave a hearty laugh. "Come on, man, don't take it so to heart. Go on, drink up."

Don Sebastián tossed off the cognac at one swallow. Between coughs he managed to bring out: "No, yes, I am happy. I have got out from under a bad mess. Let the mayor of Irola handle it now; I wash my hands of it. It was too big for me. And that damned wife of mine nagging me all day long. Renato this, Renato that. She even dreams about him, can you imagine!" He tried to laugh, but he could not bring it off.

Renato sat sunk in the upholstery of the mayor's car. He seemed stunned. Don Sebastián rode beside him in silence, wondering if it would not have been better for Sátrapa to have gone with Renato. But Sátrapa had said that it was the mayor's duty.

As they drove away from the village, Renato turned to look back, for it suddenly came to him that he might never see it again. Through the cloud of dust raised by the car he watched the houses grow smaller and smaller, and when the village disappeared from sight behind the Colina de las Angustias, he felt as though he had lost it forever. Now he realized how deeply he loved it, and he felt a great pity for it, because it was as though he had seen it sink into an abyss, as though a horrible plague of the soul had fastened upon each of its inhabitants. He had seen them peering out of their windows when he got into the car, and had seen a ripple of hatred mingled with an almost satanic joy. At that moment he had felt the hand of God falling upon the village and crushing it. And if Don Sebastián had turned toward him then, he would have seen two tears shining in Renato's eyes.

Don Jerónimo was a chain smoker of Pall Malls. Smoking was a sport that he practiced with real enjoyment. He spent long hours sitting at his desk watching the shapes the smoke took on and wondering why the smoke a newly lighted cigarette gives off is faintly blue, that of a burned-out one brownish. There was only one disappointment in this sport for Don Jerónimo, and that was that he was unable to blow smoke rings. He tried holding his mouth in every possible shape, but all that he achieved was to force the smoke out in larger or smaller puffs.

When Renato appeared in the doorway, he took a long puff and sat smiling at the ungainly figure of the switchman. Those two arms hanging limp from his shoulders, like the empty sleeves of the armless; the red patches under his eyes making him look as if he had been crying; the slightly stooped shoulders; the thick unruly hair that fell over his forehead . . . Don Jerónimo's smile became more pronounced. He was deriving a sybaritic pleasure from the scenes in store for him.

"Come in, come in," he said affably. "Please sit down."

Renato seated himself timidly. Everything had impressed him—the city with its traffic that made him fear a collision at every corner; the mayor's residence, with its great stairway; the four rooms they had crossed, with their waxed floors and the ushers with gilded buttons. And now that huge desk of magnificent wood and the overstuffed chair in which he felt as though he were swimming.

"Do you gentlemen smoke?"

Don Jerónimo held out his gold cigarette case with a magnificent gesture that further disconcerted Renato.

All he could say was: "No, no."

Don Jerónimo drew a long puff, and then said: "Very good, very good. I have been reading a lot about you. It is a beautiful thing to be a friend of God's and for Him to be among us. . . . Very good, very good. I am very happy. Don't you think we have reason to be happy?"

Renato looked at him with a tired expression, not knowing what to say to all this. He made a gesture that could, with sufficient good will, have been interpreted as assent.

The mayor went on: "Yes, Spain has always been a Catholic country. God's chosen land." And he rubbed his hands together, resting the cigarette on an ash tray in the shape of a stylized hand. A long silence followed. Then Don Jerónimo added: "Very good, very good. And

173

has God given you no message? Has he not made any . . . prophecy to you? Any . . ."

Renato had reached the apex of bewilderment. He had not seen God; he had never talked with Him. How was he going to have messages or prophecies?

Don Jerónimo watched Renato with mounting distaste. The truth was that he had not expected to encounter a rustic who did not open his mouth. He had thought the man was going to be more interesting. "At any rate," he went on, "it must be wonderful to feel that one has been chosen, called. A great . . . happiness, isn't it? When a thing of this sort happens, one must feel a . . . a great . . ."

Renato felt a sudden impulse to get up and slap the man's face. It seemed to him that the mayor was laughing at him. He put his hand to his forehead. It was damp. "I must be dizzy from the trip," he thought. And this sensation grew as he watched the mayor go on talking, talking without a stop, gesticulating, lighting another cigarette. He could not make out a word the man was saying. Then he saw Don Jerónimo take down the telephone and hold a long conversation, of which he did not grasp a word. Only at the end it seemed to him that he heard him say: "Keep well, Your Reverence. You know I am always at your command."

16

When Miguel Ponce's Lambretta pulled up in the square of Torre, the expression on the journalist's face was that of a general who has just won an important engagement. In half a minute his motorcycle was encircled by small boys. Miguelito rested his left foot on the ground, leisurely removed his goggles, folded them carefully, and put them in the upper pocket of his windbreaker. Then he ran his fingers through his tousled hair, took out a cigarette, and lighted it, shielding the match with his hand. By the time he had finished all these ceremonies, the circle had grown to two dozen, including several women.

"Is there a hotel in this place?"

Several of the boys laughed.

"Or a boarding house?"

Miguelito's temper was rising because nobody answered and one of the kids was trying to put his fingers in the exhaust.

Finally a woman said: "El Moro has a room."

"Who's El Moro?"

"The owner of the tavern. Come with me."

Six of the boys got into a fight over who should carry Miguel's bag, and six more started a race toward El Moro's house to tell him the news.

Ponce was struck by the poverty-stricken appearance of the village. All the houses were of adobe and, aside from those around the square and on the Calle de los Arcos, single-storied. And dirty and in need of paint.

At that moment a man came hurrying out of one of the houses, limping on a wooden leg that made him sway from right to left almost comically. "Oh, sir, welcome to my house. Right this way, sir, right this way."

Ponce found the obsequious tone unpleasant, but followed him. They entered the tavern, which was empty and seemed to him sordid beyond words. Glasses and pitchers were piled on the counter, and rows of dusty bottles stood on tables fastened to the walls.

"Come in, sir; you'll be as comfortable here as in your own home." The tavernkeeper talked and fawned on Ponce without stopping.

The room was small, and the only light came from a small window covered with a grating. It looked as though it was normally used as a pantry. The tavernkeeper turned on the electric light, which, as it was still day, gave a strange, wan light. The furnishings consisted of two chairs and a very high bed—later Miguel saw that it had two mattresses—over whose head hung a gory crucifix that seemed out of place in that room for some reason. Under the bed stood a big, chipped chamberpot. On a chair were a bottle of water and a thick glass that evidently had been brought up from the tavern.

When the tavernkeeper left, Miguel stood up on a chair to look out of the window. All that he could see was a dirty stableyard in which a pile of demijohns lay beside one of charcoal. A window facing him looked as though it might open on to a pigsty, of which only the roof, festooned with cobwebs, was visible.

He opened his bag, taking out of it a small typewriter, a camera, and a pad of paper, which last he put into one of his pockets. These things, a shirt, and three neckties comprised his luggage.

There was a knock at the door. "Sir, if you like, we can put your motorcycle in the stableyard."

"I'm coming."

When he got back into the tavern he asked: "Have you any cognac?"

"Yes, sir."

After his second glass of cognac, Ponce felt less marooned. He need not have felt so at all, for the whole town was thinking about him.

Miguelito had no more than set foot in the tavern when a woman had said: "I wonder if he's some sick person."

Several of the children went running home to say that a sick man had arrived.

"No, woman, he's not sick at all."

"They said sick people would be coming."

"But he's not one of them. Just take a look at him."

"You never can tell."

Later, when Ponce began to hear voices in the tavern, he left his room and saw four men sitting around a table. He greeted them: "Good day."

"Good day." They looked at him suspiciously.

"Do any of you know a—" He pulled out a notebook— "somebody called Sátrapa?"

The four men looked at one another. One of them said: "That's me." He held out his hand. "Who gave you my name?"

"Oh, the editor of *The Voice*. These hick reporters are always so stupid. They flush the bird and then don't know how to bring it down."

"Bird . . . what do you mean by bird?"

"What's happened here. The miracles."

"Oh, yes." Don César examined Miguelito more carefully. "Would you be a . . . reporter?"

"Yes, I'm on the staff of *El Día.*"

"Of Madrid?"

"Of Madrid."

A smile spread across Sátrapa's face from ear to ear. He turned to the tavernkeeper. "A round of cognac, on me." And then: "Sit down, my friend. And now tell us."

"I don't have much to tell. We saw the article in *The Voice.* The editor read it and sent me here. That's all there is to it. In Irola, the editor of that sheet gave me your name. Now you're the ones to tell me."

And Sátrapa told all. He gave Miguelito Renato's background from the time of his arrival with the circus wagon. He talked about the twenty-five years Renato had acted as switchman without having anything to do with anybody. How it had occurred to them to call on him in the matter of the cross, the confession with Father Mendizábal, and the raising of the cross.

Miguelito did not miss a word, and from time to time scribbled notes on his pad. Sátrapa had trouble telling about the raising of the cross because he was reluctant to use the word *miracle*, so he passed over it hurriedly and began to talk about the drought. Miguel kept prodding him with questions about the cross, but Sátrapa answered in monosyllables. Then he repeated over and over that the harvest had been a complete failure and that it was all Renato's fault. Whereupon Ponce, with a smile, said: "But we can't say that in the paper."

"Why not?"

"Because we have to make Renato a sympathetic figure."

"You think so?"

"If we don't make a popular hero out of him, nobody will come. We have to say that all of you worship him."

"But that's not true. . . ."

"What the devil does the truth matter!"

Sátrapa began to feel that he was on slippery ground. It was not easy for him to be a party to the farce.

"So you think that making him sympathetic . . . ?" he asked.

"They'll swarm here like flies. Day after tomorrow there will be a hundred visitors here, and in a week there'll be a thousand."

"Where in the hell are we going to put them?"

"That's up to you people. You all stand to profit. There's not going to be an empty room in the village. Every one will be rented. And you can turn any house into a boarding house. Tourists bring money with them."

"But . . ."

"It couldn't be simpler. We'll set it up well. I'll take pictures of the cross and the canary that was brought back to life. We'll make lots of copies and they'll sell like hot cakes. We can even invent a miracle-working spring— five pesetas a bottle. And rosaries, candles . . . all that stuff sells well. And things to eat—some typical kind of cake."

Martín spoke up: "Cat buns."

"Cat buns," Miguel agreed. "If you hawk them around, they'll bring in plenty. And little wooden crosses. That will be a very good item. Copying the one by the lake— crosses that fall down and come up by themselves. That's easy with a rubber band inside. See, like this: the rubber goes through the wood. Oh, you can set up quite a business here. You folks don't know what people's curiosity is like. In a couple of years not a single Spaniard will go to foreign shrines, and even the French will come here. There's nothing like novelty. You could do a good trade in canaries. 'Miracle canaries'—now there you have something original. It's too bad there isn't a relic market. If Renato were to die, that would be the payoff. 'St. Renato, the miracle-worker.' A good name, don't you think?" Miguelito got up. "But we're wasting time. I've got to do a good picture coverage. We'll have to proceed in order. First the cross, then the canary, and then the woman who was brought back to life. But first another round. Let's drink to the luck that has come to the village. Bring on the cognac."

The arrival of the Wednesday express was a sensation. Ponce, after a long-distance call to *El Día*, had prophesied that at least twelve tourists would be coming to Torre that day. His estimate fell short: there were fourteen. The first to get off the train were two women and a man in a wheelchair pushed by a boy about twenty. After him came a couple carrying a girl about twelve on a stretcher. Then two couples who seemed in perfect health but looked like foreigners. The women were the real feature of the day: they were wearing slacks! Then came Pedro Ramírez and Ricardo Lavín, of *El Tiempo* and *Correo de España*, respectively; and finally an old man wearing a goatee who was terribly pale.

Half the village was at the station, and not one child had stayed away.

"Bags . . . carry your bags, lady?"

"It's two kilometers, lady. Carry your luggage?"

"Taxi? There's none here, lady. There's my wagon."

"Two donkeys. I have two donkeys. They're gentle, sir."

"I told you we shouldn't have come. This is the end of the world."

"Help him up gently, please."

"Anyone else want to use my wagon?"

Moments later the caravan was trotting happily toward Torre de Muza.

"You wait. Tomorrow there'll be fifty," Ponce said.

"Where are we going to put them?"

"A tent business wouldn't be a bad idea. How about it, Sátrapa?"

Señora Juliana put up a sign reading: "Vacant Room." Nina put up another: "Meals Served. Thirty Pesetas." The one at Andrés's house read: "Two Rooms for Rent. Double Bed" ("Bed for Two" had been scratched out). Uncle Lucas's sign was more laconic: "Inn."

Miguelito Ponce headlined his article: "Great Multitude Visits Torre de Muza Today," and followed it up with an interview with an old man who had cancer and the mother of a girl afflicted with infantile paralysis. The first was subtitled: "I have faith," the second: "I would so love to play!"

The correspondent of *El Tiempo* headed his: "A Whole Village Fervently Gathers about the Miraculous Cross."

Ricardo Lavín in *El Correo de España:* "God Has Come Down to a Spanish Village."

Ponce sent in another article for the afternoon edition in which he said: "The government should arrange for special trains to Torre de Muza."

17 Who can claim to know the soul of a village? Peasants, being elemental creatures, are not comprehensible. They wear their hearts on their sleeves. When they love, they love; when they hate, they hate. There are no hidden crannies in them. But this, instead of making things easier, only complicates them. They veer with every changing wind. And who knows from what quarter the wind may blow tomorrow?

All Torre lived in a state of amazement. Hardly anyone ventured to express an opinion about what had happened for fear he would have to shift his position the next day. What they all felt was happiness over their state of importance. They did not know if this importance was the result of a curse or a blessing. They were just happy, without stopping to think whether they deserved to be or not.

Anyone who had observed the village objectively that Wednesday evening would have come to the conclusion that it was as when children toss a coin, heads or tails, and instead of immediately falling one way or the other, it rolls for several seconds and wavers right and left, as though it could not make up its mind, and nobody can say how it will finally fall.

At the moment it seemed to incline toward happiness, and the arrival of the visitors had given rise to an atmosphere of festivity unknown in the village since the bull-fight the year before. From all windows a smell of oil floated, and the women came to the doors of their houses with their hands covered with flour. Yes, the buns would sell well.

There was a moment of dismay when Don José Antonio refused to conduct the rosary in front of the cross. But the problem was quickly solved: Lucio would do it very well.

There was further confusion when, after the rosary, nobody knew just what the next move should be. It was clear that something had to be organized there, but what? That was the problem. The sick sat on in silence. The miracle had not occurred. Everybody was embarrassed.

But the village breathed again on seeing that the sick were not too demanding, and were willing to give God time to become aware of their presence. And, above all, the villagers gave sighs of relief when they saw that the visitors did not look too startled when asked fifty pesetas for dinner and bed for one night.

Oh, the milkmaid's dreams that sprang up in the village! Three hundred and fifty nights at fifty pesetas a night came to 17,500 pesetas. A bed was worth more than an acre of land. And needed no mules. The women smiled at the delightful figure. The men's frowns did not disappear, but at moments behind the scowls a glimmer of hope appeared. Who could say but what in the long run the drought might not prove more profitable than rain!

But the men were afraid: they knew that easy money always turns sour in the hand. But not wheat, which one sows and watches grow and ripen as though it came from one's own vitals. The men of the village loved the money

183

that came from the wheat; they knew it never went bad. But the easy money! For that reason while the women were dreaming their rosy dreams, there was a flight of crows across those of the men.

Once again morning broke dry over the village. Like a stretched hide. But that day the sun seemed to the women less merciless, and to the men less brutal. Some of the women even sang as they stripped the beds, and the radio in the tavern had been playing since morning, earlier and louder. The girls spent more time before the mirrors, and although they did not go so far as to put on their best dresses, they furbished up their everyday ones with the sashes and kerchiefs reserved for Sunday. Their mothers smiled approvingly.

Mass was better attended that day, too. Don José Antonio had received a letter from the Bishop suggesting that he take up his residence in Torre de Muza to be able to keep a closer watch on events. Thus the village enjoyed a privilege it had been denied for many months: Mass on weekdays.

Don José Antonio always said it slowly, but that day there was an air of fatigue about all his movements. The furrow that crossed his forehead was deeper, and his eyes revealed a lack of sleep. When he turned at the "*Dominus vobiscum*" and saw that more people than usual were present, he tried to feel glad, but could not. He could no longer tell which was God and which the devil. Only four days had elapsed since Don Macario's death, but how many and what difficult things had happened. He felt an oppression in his breast which made it hard for him to go on with the Mass. His arms were heavy, and it was an effort for him to move them. And when he took the wafer in his hands to consecrate it, a wave of panic came over him. He could not say why the phrase "I come not to bring peace but a sword" rose to his lips. And it was an effort for him to pronounce the words that change the bread into the body of Christ because there was a clanging of swords in his ears. And when he had said the words consecrating the chalice, his wide-open eyes stared wildly. For at that moment it seemed to him that the blood was rising and overflowing the chalice and running down the corporals to fall at his feet, and spreading to cover his shoes and ankles and running all over the church, and everyone was fleeing in terror while he stood alone before the altar and the blood rose to his waist. Then fear froze his bones, not because of what he had imagined, but because he knew that even if it happened, he could not feel more fear than he already did; that blood running through the streets would not be more terrifying than what was already running through them. But he could not say whether it was love or hate.

He had to make an almost physical effort to conclude the Mass. He felt as though a bag of sand was suspended from each of his arms, a bag from his eyes, and a bag from his soul.

When Mass was over, he sat down in the confessional, almost more out of habit than for any other reason, for on weekdays nobody in Torre went to confession. The church was practically deserted. Don José Antonio buried his head in his hands. There was only one thought in his mind: it's too much.

The wood on the right side of the confessional creaked. The priest opened the grille, and the shadow of a face appeared silhouetted against the soft clarity of the church.

"Father . . ."

He sensed the anxiety in the voice, and leaned slightly toward it.

"I need your advice."

The voice and the features that began to emerge from behind the grille revealed to him that it was María the martyr.

"Speak, daughter."

Don José Antonio became more human in the confessional. In that black well he laid off his spiritual harshness. Only his weakness remained of the priest that he was the rest of the time. He felt more vulnerable there. He spoke to the penitents hurriedly, the way that people watching beside a corpse generally speak.

"Father, you know all that is happening in this village."

"Yes, daughter. My heart is filled with fear."

"I would be happy if I were afraid. Fear is when we expect something bad. But the evil is here already. Father, the devil is in the village."

"And what can we do about it, daughter?"

"I don't know. Realize it, perhaps. Have you seen? They laugh. They live. How is that they do not see him? I feel almost as though my skin were on fire. And it is he. He."

A silence followed.

"Father, I want to ask your permission to take a vow, a vow of blood. Now I understand why I came back to life. The death I died was worthless, and God stands greatly in need of voluntary deaths. Perhaps He would like mine. Haven't you noticed how this village smells of blood? Blood is going to be shed. Why not mine?"

"Aren't you happy to be alive?"

"Father, how could I give God a life with which I was

not happy? He does not accept that which falls from one with overloaded arms, or the burdens one is longing to lay down. He likes what must be torn away, even though it carries with it a part of the flesh. Everything having to do with God verges upon death."

Don José Antonio recalled his own anxieties of a few minutes before. "I come not to bring peace but a sword," he said to himself.

And, as though she had divined his thought, she said: "When has there ever been a war that did not leave victims on both sides? War is not a game."

Don José Antonio said nothing. It was as though he was absent from the confessional.

"Then may I, Father?"

"May you what?"

"Make my vow."

Then Don José Antonio spoke, but almost without knowing what he was saying. It sometimes happened to him in the confessional that he said things he had never thought and that, once they had passed his lips, seemed to him the words of another. "Daughter, the blood you must shed is your life. Suffer, weep. Tears are the only thing that do not roil life. At times they are worth as much as blood."

"Father . . ."

"Yes, daughter?"

"I would like to ask another thing of you, to help me to come close to God. There are corners in my life that are not His. And it frightens me to think that sinners are sinners from head to foot, and we . . ."

After the woman had left, Don José Antonio felt better. He took a deep breath. And then he heard a rap to the left of the confessional. Through the grille he saw the gleam of golden hair and two hands clinging to the lattice. He heard the timid voice of a girl: "*Ave Maria Purissima.*"

Then it seemed to him that he heard a deep sigh. "Father . . ." And the voice quavered into tears.

The face withdrew for a moment, letting in enough light so Don José Antonio could recognize Magdalena.

When she had calmed down a little, she passed her hand over her eyes. "Father, I know what I am saying is foolish, but I would like to become a nun."

Don José Antonio raised his head a little and a smile came over his lips.

At this she, with a gesture as though she were going to scream, but in a low voice, said: "Don't laugh." Then, more calmly, she went on: "I have thought a lot about it."

"And what have you thought?" Don José Antonio said this tenderly, as though speaking to a child.

Her voice hoarsened. "Here we are all pigs." Then, suddenly, in a different tone: "Do you know that they wanted to kill my child?"

Don José Antonio tried to keep the tenderness, but his voice came out harsh. "Why don't you think first about your sin?"

From the other side came silence again. The girl was crying once more, but not with the hysterical tears of before. Now it was a soft, easy weeping. "Will you help me?" she asked.

It was all so simple. The girl talked like a child, relating what she had done in the tone she might have used to tell that she had stolen a handful of cookies.

"And now, what are you going to do?"

Magdalena's voice suddenly grew firmer as though she had grown years older in a second. She talked as though she had thought everything out. "When the baby is born, I will leave it in an orphanage. I will ask them to place it where I will never know about it. And then I'll enter another orphanage to look after the children of others. And perhaps one day, looking into the eyes of some child, I will wonder if it is mine."

The priest felt that the girl was painting a romantic picture of herself.

But she added sadly: "And it won't be." Then her hands clenched the grille. "But, Father, now, please, help me to protect the life of my child. Promise me that you will."

He promised.

It was after Mass that the village realized how much it needed Renato. The "program" that Torre could offer was short and unexciting. After all, tourists could not spend the day praying at the cross. Renato would have been a first-class feature.

Moreover, Don José Antonio had taken a stand, and there was no way of getting him to take part in anything. There could have been a night procession with torches—like Lourdes, according to the miller's widow —or a dawn rosary, with an ascent to the hermitage and a *Salve* before the Virgin of the Dark Eyes. But the young priest had said no, and without him little could be done.

Some of the villagers even began to speak well of Renato.

"If only Renato was here . . ."

"I always said he was a good sort."

"We're all proud of Renato here."

The children played in the streets.

"I was dead."

"And I cured you."

"Come here. You lie down here, and when I call you, you move your head like this, and then like this, and then you say: 'Where am I?' "

"All right, but tell the others to cry."

"All right, come on."

Maneras had not sent the sheep out to pasture that morning. What was the use when everything was as dry as tow? He was looking proudly at Sito, who was sitting on his lap. He had the same coarse black hair as he, and his body was beginning to look like that of a man. Only in his eyes was there a feminine touch, the only legacy Pilar had left on earth.

"I thought of asking him to bring Mother back to life, but then who would look after the little girl in heaven?"

Nicolás was afraid to answer the boy for fear the words might bring tears to his eyes. He trembled when he heard him call that lump of purplish flesh which they had laid beside the body of his wife "the little girl."

"Because Loli will still have to have milk, and maybe there are no cows in heaven. Or are there?"

"What makes you think there are no cows in heaven?"

"Because they'd make it dirty. But maybe they give her goat's milk. There must be goats. Otherwise the shepherds would have nothing to do."

Maneras ran his fingers through Sito's hair.

The boy kept repeating: "Of course, there have to be goats." Then he stopped and, opening his eyes wide, said: "And if Mother came back to life, who would teach Loli to pray? Up there they have to pray, and Loli didn't even know how to talk. And what if they wouldn't let her in because she didn't know how to pray?"

Maneras could not have said why, but talking with his son soothed his soul as the first waves of the rising tide must refresh the sweating beaches. Listening to Sito, he began to really believe in immortality.

Everything would have gone along smoothly if it had not been for that matter of Elena that morning. Definitely, neither God nor the devil was quiet in Torre.

The pilgrims, some after attending Mass, others after just a good night's rest, had set out for the cross of the lake, and after them had gone nearly all the women of the village. They gathered in groups on the little esplanade, and some began to pray while others merely waited. Not that they were waiting for anything in particular; they were just waiting. A village woman can sit down with her hands in her lap and spend hour upon hour without doing or thinking anything.

One of the praying groups, the one headed by Manuela, included Elena, the mayor's wife. She had slept badly that night and was very pale.

Manuela noticed it at once. "Are you sick?" She said it in a tone that suggested Elena had better leave, for everyone was afraid of Elena's epileptic attacks, which, though infrequent, were very violent. Several times she had begun to moan in church and had fallen to the floor with terrible convulsions.

"No, I'm all right," she had answered.

But this had not reassured Manuela, who kept watching her all the time. It was during the prayer of the fourth mystery—Jesus carrying His cross—that she suddenly got to her feet. Manuela stood up to catch her before she fell. But she did not fall. Erect and solemn, she began to walk toward the cross with her hands extended before her.

Nobody said a word, and many held their breath. Elena's eyes were glittering with an almost supernatural expression. Her small, frail body seemed invested with a new strength. They made way for her, and behind her a semicircle formed, their arms ready to break her fall. Her movements were not those of an epileptic, but measured and strong. Perhaps a little too strong.

She knelt at the foot of the cross. As though magnetized, all the women knelt behind her. From their cots the sick people raised their heads. The silence was impressive, and Elena's words could be plainly heard.

"Tell me, Lord."

There was a pause. All eyes were on Elena's lips, over which a faint tremor had come. She moved her head back and forth. She said very softly: "Yes."

She gave the impression that she was talking to someone. Her eyes were fixed on the center of the cross. The eyes of all moved from her face to the cross, trying to understand.

"As You wish, Lord."

The seconds between phrase and phrase seemed eternal. "Friday?"

They were all trying to divine the meaning of those disjointed phrases.

"I will tell him, Lord."

Elena's eyes radiated happiness. Now she was trembling from head to foot. Little by little her eyes dulled, but without losing their smile. She bent her head. All were sure that the vision had disappeared. She slowly arose from among the women, who now surrounded her on all sides. Manuela shook her by the shoulders. Elena opened her eyes as though awakening from a dream. She said in an almost childish voice: "I saw the Heart of Jesus nailed to the cross."

Many of the women turned frightened eyes on the cross, and those who had their backs to it drew away.

"What did it say to you?"

"That a great miracle will take place here on Friday. That I was to tell you."

It was then that her eyes rolled up in her head and she began to tremble. Her body fell back in Manuela's arms. It was the attack.

Once more the whole village was in a state of tension, and Miguelito Ponce headlined his report: "The Heart of Jesus Announces Great Miracle for Friday."

◆◇◆◇◆◇◆◇◆◇

18 When Renato came out of the Episcopal Palace, he was almost happy. It was about three in the afternoon, and the sun, golden and beautiful, gave luster to the city asphalt. As he still had an hour before train time, he decided not to go directly to the station, but to let his feet choose the route they preferred. They led him along a gently sloping street that opened into a small irregular square where he

encountered his first surprise. Colored lights were strung like a ceiling over the square. It was then that he realized that Irola was having a celebration.

He stopped and looked at them for a long time. "How pretty!" The yellow were combined with the red, green, and blue, giving the effect of a great colored tree whose trunk was the fountain in the center of the square. At night it must be beautiful! For a moment he was tempted to stay there overnight just to see them lighted. But then he laughed at his own nonsense. He had to content himself with closing his left eye and imagining how they would shine in the dark.

The city was still drowsing, and the first customers were straggling toward the cafés. It gave Renato pleasure to watch the passers-by, especially if they were wearing bright colors. When the girls went by, he never looked at what most people did, but half closed his eyes and watched the fluttering of their dresses. He looked at the crowds as though at a landscape, as though seeing them from a tower.

Now he realized that there were colored lights in one of the side streets, too, and turned down it. He half closed his eyes again to see them, and they seemed to him like huge strings of crullers hanging from a wire. He laughed. Then the lights took on the shape of an arc, and all together seemed a corridor of colors. A sign read: "To the Fair Grounds."

He walked along under the arches until he came to a little garden flanked by two rows of trees that partly covered it overhead. It gave Renato the impression of a nest. But then he was not sure whether it was because of the interlacing branches or because of the gaiety within. Groups of children were running along the walk under the two rows of trees while others went up and down the slides or played on the swings in the middle.

Now Renato realized that his happiness was not groundless. He would not have dreamed that there could be places as gay as this. He thought to himself: "When I come to the city, I'll spend all my spare time here." And added: "Because they'll let me go out of the monastery. I'm not going to be a friar."

He sat down on a bench, and half a minute later a little boy hid behind him. "Ready," he shouted.

But apparently the whole place was a box of surprises. At that very moment a band struck up behind him. He jumped up, half frightened, and saw that the boy who had been hiding behind him had forgotten his game and was rushing toward the iron fence that separated the garden from the street. "The circus, the circus, the circus!"

Renato followed him and pressed his face against the wire of the fence. A procession preceded by a group of youngsters was approaching. Six men dressed in red and yellow walked in front playing the drum and cymbals. Then three more, wearing outfits that Renato could not identify, came riding prancing roan horses. They wore broad felt hats, and from their shoulders and down the horses' flanks yards of rope hung. It surprised him, too, to see that they were wearing shining pistols at their belts. Then the wonder, the incomparable feature: behind the horses came an elephant, no less. It seemed to Renato that he was in heaven.

At this point the children, who had been watching the parade beside him, started to run, almost between his legs, and nearly knocked him down. "Come on, let's follow them." Renato did not give it another thought, and a minute later he was running with the children. He did not notice how two girls laughed at the clumsy way he ran.

The elephant walked slowly and rested its whole body on each foot as it set it down. Renato was thinking: "If it brought it down on anyone . . ." On the elephant's back there was a little colored house, just as in story books, and from its windows a man dressed like a Hindu threw colored streamers to right and left. Renato was soon down among the children, picking them up, and in a few minutes his hands were full of colored paper. He put them in his pocket without looking at them, and went on gathering them up until his pockets were stuffed.

The parade was now entering the square of Irola, and when Renato noticed that the hands of the clock were almost on four, he remembered for the first time that he had to make the train. The train left in seven minutes, and he did not even know where the station was. Fortunately, it was not far off, and when he came up onto the platform panting, he could hear the puffing of the engine. He drew a long breath as he heard the whistle. "Made it." The train pulled out.

The Bishop of Irola spent the afternoon more quietly. He had hit upon the perfect solution. After four days of questioning—and this morning's session had lasted for three hours—he had come to the conclusion that it was impossible to reach any conclusion. The waters in this business were turbid, and too many passions were involved. He would have had to go to Torre himself to study the problem *in situ*, and could have arrived at some conclusion only after talking with the entire village. But that would only have made matters worse. Conflicting groups would have sprung up, and hatred would have been engendered in hearts that were still unpoisoned. The fact of the crop failure could not be ignored.

As a result, he had decided that the only thing that could resolve the matter was to wait and at the same time remove Renato from the village. Then, after six months, when hate had disappeared and a new harvest had cleansed the hearts, would come the moment to undertake a serene investigation.

So he had found Renato a job as gardener in the near-by Augustine convent and had forbidden him to reveal his true identity in the capital. Renato had accepted this plan with real delight, a fact that had reassured the Bishop. He had only one slight twinge of conscience. He had invited Renato to have lunch with him, and during the meal he had felt strangely communicative and had told him almost his whole life story. Now His Excellency asked himself what had impelled him to confess to a stranger, and he could find no answer. He was reassured by his remembrance of Renato's eyes as he had listened, like the eyes of a child listening to a fairy story.

The Bishop was thinking all this during his evening visit to the altar. Mingled with his prayers like gusts of wind were scraps of his talk with Renato, as, for example, when Renato had confessed that for a long time he had been unable to sleep because his dreams were poisoned, and the several nights he had got up because he had seen the whole village on fire. The Bishop recalled one phrase that surprised him by its exactitude: "I do not work miracles. Someone throws them out from inside me." And that other: "Is the flint to blame for having fire in it? Let them not strike me if they don't want sparks." Their dialogue came to his memory:

"Are you better since all this began?" he had asked.

"Yes, sir, I think so," was the answer. The tone was humble.

"In what do you notice this?"

"Now I know how to suffer without complaining."

The answer had surprised the Bishop, and he had asked: "Do you suffer much?"

"Your Reverence, Christianity is not a lollipop." He had said this laughing, as though it were a joke. But the Bishop had understood the deadly seriousness in the words.

The Bishop wondered why he had then asked him that other question, but he had felt compelled to know. "My son, tell me: have you committed any mortal sin during your life?"

Renato had not answered, but he had thrown his head back.

The Bishop, fearing he might have been tactless, then said: "Don't answer if you don't want to."

"I want to, Your Reverence," Renato had answered with simplicity, "but I am afraid I will be committing one if I say no. And, yet, that would be the truth."

The Bishop recalled all this now like a nightmare remembered in the light of day. His lips moved in prayer. And a minute later he realized that he was praying for the switchman.

When Renato had caught his breath, he began to look around for a seat in one of the compartments. As he was opening the door, he was almost knocked down by a young girl as tall as a vaulting pole and dressed in bright green. She was leading a group of a dozen other girls who were laughing and talking all at the same time.

"Let's take this other one. This is full of . . ."

"Isn't that first class?"

"Who's got the tickets?"

"Did you find out if there's a river in the village?"

"If there isn't, there's the lake."

"Oh, lakes have a foul smell."

"Who's got the lunches?"

"Did Roberto finally decide to come?"

The girls were all crowded on the platform because they could not open the door between the cars. Renato was squeezed into a corner.

"It's locked."

"That's just lovely."

"We can stay here."

"Well, here we can sing."

"Ask somebody if there's a river in Torre."

Renato spoke up. "No, there's no river."

"Are you sure?" The girl who asked the question was small and heavily made up.

"I come from there."

"And there isn't any?"

"No."

Twelve mouths gave an identical "Oh" of disappointment.

"We can eat our lunch anywhere."

"You wait and see what fun we have."

"Maybe we'll bring back a miracle."

"My gum boil."

"Or my boy friend."

"Or mine."

Four voices and seven peals of laughter.

"What's the name of the new saint? Does anybody know?"

"Ask that man."

Renato was questioned about the name of "the new saint." He looked at them in astonishment. "New saint?"

"Yes, that fellow in Torre."

Renato had no idea what they were talking about. He tried to excuse himself. "I . . . I . . ."

But the girls were no longer listening to him.

"Look at that house!"

They all turned their heads.

"With a swimming pool!"

"Isn't it darling!"

"So Roberto didn't come."

Renato had managed to slip away, and he was still asking himself what they had meant by "the new saint of Torre." That day he did not feel the ground under his feet. He was happy, and the memory of all that had happened during the preceding months had faded away. He smiled, thinking: "What children they are," and then added: "They remind me of butterflies." And they really did, in their galaxy of colors.

He slid back the door of the first compartment.

"Oh, excuse me."

Two sick women were stretched out on the two lengthwise seats. From beside the window a young woman in a nurse's uniform turned and smiled.

In the next compartment there was an empty seat. Across from Renato a stout woman fanned herself steadily. Beside him, a fair-haired girl leaned over a boy wearing black glasses who answered without turning his head toward her. Renato realized that he was blind.

The woman across from him asked: "Are you sick, too?"

"Me?" And he thought to himself: "What strange questions people ask me today!" "No," he answered. "No, I'm all right."

"Ah!" The lady looked disappointed. "But you're going to Torre."

"Yes."

"What for?"

A little old man at the end of the row laughed at the woman's insistence.

Renato hardly knew what to answer. "I . . . am going . . . I live there."

"That's wonderful. Now you can tell us about the things that have been happening there." But evidently the lady did not want to listen, but to talk herself. She babbled on: "It's just marvelous what has happened, isn't it? I had always wanted Spain to have a miracle-working shrine. It was a shame for every other place to have them and not us. And here, so near . . . I'm so excited. And we need one so badly. Haven't you noticed the state things are in? Have you seen those girls? Wouldn't you think they'd be ashamed to dress that way? Not a scrap of a sleeve on any one of them." Renato now realized that they were all bare-armed. "And those low necks! A judgment of God, that's what we deserve. Or they deserve. Absolutely shameless. Oh, if I were God . . ." Renato shuddered at the thought of what the world would be like with a God as stupid as she.

The woman suddenly stopped talking, and turned to Renato. "But I interrupted you. You were going to tell us about the village. Because you must have seen the miracles. Oh, it must have been marvelous. To see the cross arise. Such a pretty miracle. And what is he like?"

"He?"

"Yes, the man of God."

"The priest? He died."

"No, not the priest. I mean that man. Yes, indeed, a man of God! You find such beautiful souls among the peasants . . . where you least expect it. . . . Yes, diamonds in the mud. I want to see him and get him to speak before our Association. Oh, you must excuse me. I haven't introduced myself. I am the president of . . ."

Renato no longer took in anything that she was saying. He was dizzy and had such a feeling of nausea that he could not hear anything. What reached his ears was a noise like the pounding of the surf mingled with a few disjointed words. For the woman talked, talked, went on talking:

"Blah, blah, devotion, blah, blah, hell, miracles, mercy, rosary, charity, Christianity, blah, blah, most Catholic country in the world, foreign fashions, blah, blah, corruption, Communism, perverted youth, blah, blah, the way they dress, blah, blah, San Melifades, blah, blah, when I was young, communion every day, blah, blah, poor, charity, don't appreciate, blah, blah, what have they got to complain about, blah, blah . . ."

Renato managed to say: "Please excuse me: I'm a little dizzy."

He went into the corridor and put his head out of the window. A gust of wind struck him in the face, but instead of helping, it only made his nausea worse. The woman slapped him on the back, but that only made him dizzier. He finally felt what he had eaten coming up, and a hot stream trickled down his chin, dirtying the window glass.

He did not hear the screech of one of the girls. Nor the other's answer.

"How revolting!"

"Why didn't he go into the toilet?"

He felt better, and the air refreshed him. He was very pale, and still a little dizzy. He did not notice the gesture of the woman, who was feeling around for a handkerchief in the leather bag on her arm. Nor did he see her hesitate for a moment with the handkerchief in her hand and then put it back in the bag.

"Wipe off your chin," she said. "Don't you have a handkerchief?"

Renato did as she said, and tried to smile. "Thank you."

"Don't mention it. You've eaten something that disagreed with you. You'll be all right now. Always when your stomach is upset you don't feel right until you . . ."

She went on talking, now from her seat in the compartment. Renato stayed beside the window. It was then that he discovered that his discomfort was not physical, but something much deeper. It was fear. He was beginning to discover the truth, and it frightened him.

He walked a little way down the corridor, and convinced himself that he was not mistaken as he saw more invalids in the other compartments. He returned to the window, and had the feeling that he was going to faint. He leaned his head against the pane, which felt oddly cold, considering how hot it was.

Tears rose to his eyes. "This is the end," he thought. "This was all that was needed, the miracle fair. How can

You stand it? Nobody believes, nobody. Or perhaps they believe, but none of them loves."

He felt alone. But his loneliness was not that of a person who feels nobody beside him; it was a far deeper loneliness, that of a man naked in the face of emptiness, such loneliness as we shall feel at the hour of judgment, completely alone before God. Everything around him—objects, time, events—was falling, collapsing. He felt as though his whole life had been laid in the balance and that all was staked on a single instant. He passed sentence: lost. He saw himself as totally useless—even worse, as harmful. "Everything would have been easier without me," he thought. "I am a stumbling-block." His soul gave a gesture whose physical counterpart would have been to raise his eyes, saying: "I am in Your way."

What he felt now was vertigo. He would have liked to fall, to be like the others, to live. To be able to be bad, to be able to hate. Ah, the longing he had to strike out, to kill, to do anything so long as it was evil. And then rest and say: "There, now I am like the others, like all of them. Now I can live."

"It is impossible to live and be with You. It is very dangerous." Yes, he had staked everything on the good, and that always had to be paid for. It was not that it pained him. He knew suffering and was not afraid of death. But he had never suspected the scope of the forces of evil. For them to hate him, insult him, kill him, that was natural. But to call him a saint, no. To demand miracles of him, no. To believe in him, no.

That was why he was afraid. "The real flouting of God is not hating Him. It is making a puppet of him for our own ends. Hatred aggrandizes the object of hatred. The

smiling lie, there is the enemy." And now he was surrounded by lies on all sides.

Sweat was trickling down his forehead, and he felt in
his pocket for his handkerchief. His hand touched something hard and crackling and he pulled it out. It was a
ball of paper. At first, not knowing what it was, he un-
folded it slowly: the circus program. The blown-up picture of a clown filled the center. Underneath, the name:
Jimmy. It was not a funny face, but a happy one. Two
enormous ears, a wide mouth, prominent cheekbones.
The eyes were blue, and their placidity was emphasized
by two blue spots in the inner corners. The brows rose
over the eyes like two arches. The shining bald head displayed a little yellow hat where the nonexistent hair
should have been.

In that face Renato divined his own calling. That was
what he was, a clown, a man who knew how to juggle six
balls. That was what he should always have been; he was
good for nothing else. And wasn't it enough to make the
world laugh? Now what he was doing was making it suffer. He felt responsible for all Torre's sufferings, for all
the infirmities of those traveling in that car. Responsible, above all, for the new suffering that all of them
would pile on his back that day. Disappointment is worse
than a cancer.

He crumpled up the program angrily and went to lower
the window to throw it out. Then he saw that he was
not alone. Beside him stood the blonde girl and the blind
boy.

"Tell me what you see."

The girl, who was herself little more than a child, put
her arm around the boy's neck and leaned down to whisper

in his ear, perhaps because she felt that their conversation was ridiculous to all except the two of them. Renato listened carefully.

"There's a big field with hills in the background. We just passed a little house. It had flower pots in the window. We are also passing many telegraph poles. And here comes a grove where there are horses grazing."

"What color are they?"

"All colors. White, roan; there's a black one."

"Which are there the most of?"

"White ones. And now a river."

"A big one?"

"No, a little one."

"Are there women washing in it?"

"Yes, two."

"I like rivers. I remember those of the Nativity. I like them. You feel cool when you imagine them. What else?"

"Now a flock of pigeons."

"How pretty!"

Renato was disturbed. The light was growing in him again. He followed the pigeons with his eyes. Then he closed his eyes and they went on flying about his soul. It was like a river of peace.

"Are you brother and sister?" he asked.

The girl had eyes that brought peace, too, the same as imagining a flock of pigeons. Renato could not have said what color they were. He only knew that they were pure. That was enough.

"Are you going to Torre?"

The girl nodded again.

"How long has he been blind?"

"For the last two years. It was cancer, and they had to remove his eyes."

"And he's going to Torre to . . ." Renato felt his fear coming back. Now he was not afraid for himself. Not even for God. He was afraid for the child. For all the children in the world. He squatted down until his face was level with that of the boy, and said, almost crying: "Don't go, don't. May God preserve your blindness." And then, pleadingly: "Why do you want to see?"

"Isn't the world beautiful?"

The boy's voice was as clear as his sister's eyes.

Renato answered by nodding his head, but then remembered immediately that the boy was blind. "It is beautiful when you are five," he said, "but not when you grow up. No, ask God not to cure you. That will be the real miracle. The pigeons inside you are more beautiful than those outside, believe me."

Renato stood up. Pointing to the boy, he asked the girl: "What is his name?"

"Juan Carlos."

"And yours?"

"Maísa."

"Tell me, do you love him?"

"Love who?"

"Your brother."

She laughed.

"Then listen to me. If you love him, don't let him go to Torre. Stay at the station and take the first train back."

"But . . ."

"Pay attention to one who knows. The only thing you will take away from Torre is sorrow. Pay attention to me: alongside the station there is a meadow. Sit down in it and say the rosary. And go back on the first train."

The girl looked at him without understanding. She was

about to say something when she was interrupted by the shrieking of the girls.

"We're there."

"What a crummy station!"

"Where's the town?"

"We can't even see it."

"And Roberto didn't come?"

◆◆◆◆◆◆◆◆◆◆

19   When the train stopped at the platform in Torre, Renato knew that his hour had come. He felt weak, and nausea once more filled his mouth. He drew back from the window to let the stout woman by.

"I can't go into the village. I'll stay on the train till everybody is off. Then I'll tell the stationmaster I'm leaving, and I'll go back to the city on the mixed train. For good."

He went into the lavatory to gain time. The trains had never stopped this long in Torre. It was a break for the crew because they were able to get down and stretch their legs. They were talking.

"You'll have to introduce me to her."

"Like hell I will. So you can doublecross me?"

"She like to be loved up?"

"A little bit."

"Only a little bit?"

"Not enough to suit me."

They both laughed.

That day the unloading of the sick was slower. The village lads acting as porters did not have a clear idea of what they were supposed to do. The nurses shouted their heads off, giving orders that nobody obeyed.

"I'd like to stay here a day and see one of those miracles."

"What would you ask for? For the girl friend to be a little more obliging?"

"You dope."

The two engineers laughed, slapping each other on the back.

"Did you see the bunch of girls that got off?"

"They didn't appeal to me. Too stuck up."

"You know all about them, don't you? How about teaching me?"

"Teach you? Mathematics is what I'll teach you. Or why don't you ask the saint?"

Finally the last of the sick seemed to have got off. The small fry swarming around the station had disappeared, and very few persons remained on the platform.

"O.K. Let's go."

When the train was about to pull out, Renato got off. There was nobody in the station, for which he was thankful. He was just going out of the door when someone called to him.

"Listen."

He hesitated a moment before turning back. It was the voice of a girl and it sounded familiar to him. He turned around. It was the girl who had been on the train.

"My brother hasn't stopped crying."

"Where is he?"

"In the waiting-room. Here."

He went in. It was very dark, and for a moment he could see nothing. Someone called him by his name.

"Are you here, Renato?"

He made out a figure beside the boy. "I can't see a thing." Finally he recognized María the martyr. "Oh, it's you."

But he did not go toward her, but toward the boy, whose face was sorrowfully puckered. It was his way of crying. He had no other.

"I want to go to the cross. Why won't you take me?"

Renato knelt down beside him. "What for? The cross would only make you suffer. Crosses are only for dying. They are only for that."

"I want to go."

"You should not go."

And now Renato began to be afraid. There was a scent as of miracles. His heart was throbbing as on earlier occasions. He said almost in a scream: "No, not that!"

The three eyed him in amazement.

"What did you say?"

But they understood that he was not talking to them. He was looking upward. "Thanks," he said.

Then he bent down toward the boy. "Juan Carlos, you don't know what life is like. I do. For that reason I can promise you that you will be happy because you are good. You don't have to see to live contented."

He stopped, and suddenly his face lit up. "Don't you see the cross?" he asked the boy.

"Where?"

"Within you. Look well. It is large. Of stone. It stands beside a lake. To one side there is a wall. It is the cemetery wall. There a path begins, a path lined with green trees that leads to a shrine. You see it? You see it all?"

The boy nodded. "Yes, it's all just as you have said."

"Now, are you happy? Your cross is more beautiful than that of the village."

The boy nodded again. "And who are you?" he asked.

"A man from here, from the village."

"Aren't you the man of the miracles?"

"No, not I."

"What is your name?"

"What does it matter? Call me what you like."

"When I think about you, to me you will be 'the good man.' Do you like that?"

"I like it. And now go. You'll be cooler outdoors."

The children went out and Renato was left alone with María the martyr. He was tired and sat down on one of the benches along the wall. He buried his head in his hands and remained silent. María watched him without venturing to talk, and the silence grew heavier as the minutes passed. Dusk would soon be falling. The sun, its glow faded, drew a line through the room, dividing it.

Finally María spoke. "Why did you come?"

Renato did not move.

She went on: "You should not have come. This is a hell. He has entered many souls."

"He? Who?"

"The Evil One. Satan."

The ray of sunlight paled and then disappeared.

"We are in his hands. All of us."

Renato raised his head and saw her eyes gleaming in the shadow. As though they had been flayed.

"I couldn't stand it any more. I was going. You cannot understand, Renato"—she was crying now—"what this is like. It was horrible before, but now . . . They all mock God. They peddle buns in his name. Isn't that monstrous! And they are happy. Yesterday there were forty visitors; today there must have been about two hundred. They talk of nothing but money. Because these people spend money. They pay as much as a hundred pesetas for a night's lodging. And . . ."

"Are there still more horrors?"

"Two women have come from the capital."

"Two women?"

"Yes, two . . ."

Renato understood why his heart had hurt when he got off the train.

She went on: "I couldn't stand any more. I ought to stay, but . . . I can bear it for César to be untrue to me, but not when he does it almost in the name of God. He talks about Him now. He befouls His name. And that I cannot bear."

"Yes, filth is disgusting, but what is really diabolical is the lie."

Renato felt as though his head were splitting, as though a murky fog had entered it and was solidifying inside. He got up. "Let's go."

"They'll kill you."

"If it has to be . . ." He spoke the words very slowly. "Let's go."

A fresh evening breeze was beginning to stir the fields as they went out. To the right of the road there was a trough with a faucet.

"Excuse me," Renato said. He put his head under the stream of water and held it there for some time. Then he let the water drip off and ran his open fingers through his hair. He stood up, and the water ran down his face and shirt. Then he wore a broad smile. "Let's go."

He remembered María Belén.

"Were you going without the child?"

"No, she's in the pine grove with the other children. I came ahead to get the tickets. There she comes."

The child had seen them, and came running with that gait which seemed as if it would shake her body apart. Renato had a feeling of distress as he watched her; he realized for the first time that there was something tragic about that puppet-like figure coming toward them. But he also noticed that as the girl came nearer to them the anxiety he felt began to fade; it disappeared completely when she was two yards off. He realized that this difference depended on whether one could see her eyes or not, and it frightened him for a moment to think that if she were to go blind she would be a monster.

But this thought lasted only a second, for the girl had thrown herself at him and was hugging and kissing him without saying a word. He, too, hugged her in silence. They looked into each other's eyes, laughing. It was not until then that the girl said: "I'm so glad you came." Then, after a silence: "I was afraid."

"Afraid? Of what?"

But the girl did not answer. She had got down and was running ahead of them.

In the meantime most of the "pilgrims" had reached the village. Some of them had been lucky enough to grab one of the four ramshackle taxis that had come to Torre on the scent of good business. The wrangling over the cars would have put Renato in a bad humor, but fortunately he did not witness it. He would have seen "Madame President of Such-and-Such an Association" arguing with a nurse about who had got there first. "Madame President" said that she had opened the righthand door first. The nurse said she had opened the lefthand one first. "Madame President" answered that that was enough of such nonsense, and first come, first served. The taxi-driver said they were holding him up and that he could have been to town and back. "Madame President," firmly settled in the back, said she was not moving from there and knew her rights. The nurse slammed the door, muttering something about charity. "Madame President" said that charity begins at home. She also said that she had never seen such a dirty car, and that it was an outrage the way the taxi-drivers were taking advantage of people and that they had no right to charge thirty pesetas for a two-kilometer drive. Later "Madame President" descended in a dignified manner from the cab and devoutly arranged a veil over her head.

Not all had been so lucky. Some of them had had to wait in the shade of the pine grove for the taxis to come back, or had decided to make the trip on foot or in wagons. But all of them, sooner or later, had been accosted by Lucio.

"Bed, a bed for the night? Who wants a bed for the night?"

This had been one of Miguelito Ponce's bright ideas, syndicating the innkeepers. To spare the pilgrims the troublesome search for lodgings, it had been decided that all who had available beds would give their names to Lucio, who would take charge of apportioning the occupants in order of priority.

"With meals?"

"Dinner only."

"Calle del Cristo, Number 14."

"Lodgings? First class, sir? Calle de las Monjas, 4."

"Lodgings?"

Renato and María walked along in silence. Neither did María Belén talk. Renato felt gone again. That sensation of inner emptiness which had preceded the miracles was becoming more pervading. He walked like an automaton, and thought and felt as though someone else was directing him. María respected his silence. She looked at him and felt him so wonderfully different and distant. Besides, it was no effort for her to be quiet. She had spent so many years that way! But whereas Renato felt his head empty, María's was bursting with ideas. Ideas that, besides, were absurd. Why did she have the feeling that she was ascending Calvary? It was a foolish idea, but she could not get rid of it.

"Nobody is going to die here," she said out loud without realizing what she was saying.

She was afraid that Renato might have heard her, but he had not moved a muscle and went striding along with his hands in his pockets. It was hard for María to keep up with him. María Belén, too, had fallen behind and was having trouble following them. María thought to herself that the child had walked a lot that day. But she did not venture to say anything to Renato, for he seemed so withdrawn.

When they reached the village, Renato stopped for a moment. María had the feeling that time, too, had stopped. But his indecision lasted only a few seconds. Suddenly he turned sharply toward the Calle de las Monias, and his first step had something memorable about it for María. It was as though the village had sensed Renato's presence. Several doors and windows opened, and everyone felt caught up in the magnetism that was drawing Renato. There was no previous accord, and yet all joined that procession. Some of the men left what they were

doing; frying pans were quickly removed from the fire.
Renato walked fast, and scarcely anyone could keep up
with him. He was some two yards ahead of María, who
followed him with bowed head, alone, too. And two
yards behind her came a group that grew more numerous
each minute. María Belén had disappeared from sight in it.

The silent procession moved in an almost solid cloud of
dust. The sun had set, and the clarity of the afternoon
was diffused. The men looked at one another as though
asking what was going to happen. Renato's eyes were
hard and impenetrable. His arms hung parallel to his
body. He was deathly pale. His pace was rapid and he was
well ahead of the group, which from time to time trot-
ted to keep from falling too far behind. María had been
swept up by the group, ahead of which Renato now
moved alone.

At an intersection a dog came out and barked for a
long time at those going by. Every head was turned
as though warning him to be quiet. Someone threw a
stone at him, and the animal made off, howling lugubri-
ously.

Renato stopped for a second and ran his hand over his
forehead. Many of the crowd imitated him. They realized
that it was hot. Several of the women wiped their hands
on their aprons.

As they came near the cross, the sound of "Hail Marys"
reached the crowd's ears. After the "Holy Mary" there
was a silence. Many instinctively moved their lips to say
a "Hail Mary" in the interval, but stopped before doing
so.

At the turn that led directly to the little esplanade,
Renato stopped for a moment, and with him, the procession. Some approached him cautiously. They saw how his

lower lip was trembling and how his right fist clenched as his chin jutted forward. He was breathing deeply. He turned the corner.

The little esplanade was almost full. If Renato had been able to see, he would have recognized in one corner the girls who had been on the train, all of them wearing jackets now. Fourteen cots were lined up before the cross. Kneeling beside them, several nurses were praying. Behind and to the sides were about a hundred of the villagers. He could have seen Manuela, Sátrapa, and the twins.

All that Renato saw was Lucio kneeling on the second step of the cross, while he prayed in a voice like that of a schoolboy: "Hail Mary, full of grace, the Lord is with thee, and blessed is the fruit . . ." He stopped, hearing the oncoming procession, turned his head and stood crouched in a ridiculous posture, neither kneeling nor erect.

All eyes turned toward Renato. The silence grew tense. Those who had followed him fanned out in a semicircle and stretched their necks to see what was going to happen.

Renato moved forward, and the crowd stepped aside to let him by. He walked slowly, with measured step, like a somnambulist. The few seconds it took him to reach the cross seemed interminable. Sweat was pouring down every forehead, but nobody thought of wiping it off. Renato's teeth were set, and the bones of his jaw stood out.

He went up to the cross and mounted the first step, where Lucio still crouched in his ridiculous posture. He turned toward all and stood gazing at them with the look of a person who sees nobody. His eyes were dull and his pallor was intense. He looked as though he was going to have a seizure.

But suddenly his face reddened, his eyes began to glow, and his fist lashed out against Lucio's jaw. Lucio rolled down the steps like a rag doll. Without a groan. Without a word.

"Stand still!"

All eyes turned toward the man who had spoken. It was Sátrapa. He had gone up to the cross and was less than two yards from Renato.

As though he had been wounded by fire, Renato leaped upon Sátrapa and the two rolled to the ground, Don César on the bottom. The labored breathing of both could be heard, and the word "snake, snake," repeated over and over by the switchman. Sátrapa's face was congested, and he was struggling helplessly to free himself from the grasp of Renato, who now lifted his fist and drove it mercilessly into Don César's face once, twice, twenty times. "Snake, snake," he kept saying. Sátrapa screamed like a child and threshed about like a clumsy animal. A ring had formed around them. Everyone was silent.

Then Don César's strength seemed to leave him, and he stopped struggling. At this Renato got up, looked at those around him with that absent air, and wiped his face with the back of his hand. "Leave me alone," he said.

They made way for him and he went off, all eyes following him.

On the ground Sátrapa was making vain efforts to get up.

20

The forerunner of tragedy is not tumult, but silence. And silence had taken possession of that village. Sátrapa got up without saying a word, brushed off his clothes, from which a cloud of dust arose, took a handkerchief out of his pocket, and wiped his face. He did not utter a word, but his eyes were those of a person who has reached a decision.

None of those around him said a word, either. They looked at one another in silence, as though afraid to make mutual confession of their hatred. They did not know how to voice it, but there was in all of them the calm that precedes an explosion. They averted their eyes from one another, fearful lest what in reality all were thinking should be manifest.

It was a strange procession that wound up the Calle de las Monjas. Those house fronts, which knew by heart the air of those who accompany and return from funerals, must have seen that this was a very different thing. Small groups had formed, some of which moved with heads bowed while others talked of trifling matters. In a doorway a woman was crying, softly, silently. In the tavern, Martín, on the other hand, was having an attack of hysterical laughter which would suddenly break off, only to start up again, harsh and grating.

The evening air had grown heavy, but nobody seemed

aware of the brewing storm. Every throat was dry with dust. The house fronts seemed more dun than ever before, and all the windows were opening up, one after the other.

The only ones left before the cross were the "pilgrims." Nobody had told them anything, but they all realized that "he" was involved. And that they had made a mistake, or, rather, that they had been cheated. Yes, they all felt that they had been the victims of a fraud, a fraud in bad taste.

Someone had said there was a return train soon, and nobody needed a minute to make up his mind to take it. They all tore up the slips of paper that gave them the right to have dinner and sleep in such and such a house. The ground was littered with scraps of colored paper.

Silence prevailed among them at the station, too, except for the girls, who had taken out their lunch and were eating it there. At first they ate and looked around them silently, but then laughter began to spread from one face to another until it broke out in nervous gaiety of the sort that one knows is forbidden, but which perhaps for that very reason is sweeter. María Jesús gave an imitation of Lucio in front of the cross, and Maísa pretended that she was going to slap her face. But all the others looked at them reprovingly, and they went outdoors. From time to time the sound of their laughter could be heard, and the effect on the sick people was like that of a dentist's drill.

A sigh of relief went up as the train pulled into the station. If the crew had been the same, they would have noticed the difference of expression in those they had seen get off and those who got on now. But the men running the train noticed nothing, for they were interested only in arguing the relative merits of Kubala and Di Stefano.

The train pulled out. And its departing whistle aroused

in every house of Torre the feeling that a skin was being ripped off.

Renato sat with his head in his hands, trying to reconstruct the afternoon's happenings, but he could make no sense of them. His head did not ache; it felt as though it was not there. On the other hand, he felt his heart perfectly. He knew that he loved, but whom? It was so difficult. Perhaps he had never felt so close to men as at this moment. And to God? He had never known too much about Him. He had been a good man, that was all. He did his best to understand why all these things were happening to him. And the only conclusion he could reach was that he would never understand.

Someone opened the door of his house. Renato did not even raise his head. He felt the coolness in the air. Whoever had come in sat down beside him in silence. And Renato soon forgot the presence in the room. But he did notice that he felt better, cooler, more contented. Almost happy. He felt the need to express his gratitude, but did not raise his head.

When Lucio entered the house, Manuela wanted to say something to him, but she was afraid to. He had dropped into a chair almost without looking at her. She saw that he was nervous, undecided, like a man thinking about something which he cannot make up his mind to do. Suddenly he got up, went to the door, and opened it quickly. Then he paused, standing for several seconds with his hand on the knob. Then he closed it slowly, and dropped back in the chair.

The old woman looked at the pile of buns on the table and said: "Dear God, dear God."

2 2 1

The gray twin came and went from the bed to the cupboard. She was folding sheets and spreads with incredible speed. The blue twin watched her come and go, and shook her head from left to right. Then she sighed deeply.

Sátrapa caressed his shotgun as he cleaned it. This was his one consolation. His hatred, bigger than he was, overflowed his heart. Besides, he was full of fear. Now he realized that he should have put an end to this earlier. For the worst of it all was that now he was fully convinced that Renato was a good man. He did not know why he thought this now, but he did. What he had in mind was not an adventure, but a crime. He felt a dirty pleasure as he realized this. Killing a guilty person must be an utter bore.

What made him most ashamed was what had just happened to him with Matilde. His mind was nailed to the cross, and that had acted as a curb-bit on his sensuality.

The thought of her future frightened Matilde. But deep in her heart she felt that she had been freed. She drove away her unpleasant thoughts and managed to fall asleep.

María Belén, sitting beside Renato, watched him without being able to make up her mind to speak to him. She was still frightened by all that had happened. Frightened, but happy.

Julián hit the fence with the willow switch he was carrying in his hand. He bit a piece of loose skin off his lower lip and gave a kick to a bucket, which echoed hollow as it hit the stones. "All that was ridiculous. Why couldn't they live in Torre the same as in other villages? Work and bread, that was all they needed. And after that, perhaps, God." He banged a gate and set out toward the tavern.

María the martyr was praying in the church. Today, for some reason, her prayer came tumbling out. She was afraid, with a diffuse, deep fear.

Lucio left his house and made for Sátrapa's. But then he changed his mind, going instead to the sacristy, where he began to fold up the chasubles. But he stopped doing it almost at once. Everything wearied him that night.

Uncle Lucas was casting up accounts of money he had advanced. He would not be the one who lost the most. His worry was the trouble he was going to have collecting.

Renato said to María Belén: "But why does all this happen to me?" María Belén looked at him with wide eyes, but said nothing. "I am afraid," he said. And two rivulets of sweat ran down his face.

Sátrapa was shaving in front of the mirror. He was slow and awkward. But then he saw a smile begin behind the lathered face. He let himself laugh. He needed to.

Lucio let the lid of the vestment chest fall. "Why not?"

Julián walked into the tavern. He said to Martín: "A good night to get drunk."

María the martyr said: "And deliver us from evil, Amen."

Manuela watched Lucio come out of the sacristy. She saw him hesitate again at the door. "Cowards, cowards," she thought.

María Belén said: "I will pray for you."

Satrapa looked into the mirror with a strained smile. " 'Snake!' You're going to choke on that."

223

María the martyr said: "Now and in the hour of our death. Amen." And went back to her house. She was trembling.

El Moro said: "Two coming up."

Sátrapa counted: one, two, three . . . up to twenty-five. Then he waited a moment. He raised his eyes and riveted them on Lucio's. "And the balance when the job's done. Is that right?"

"That's right."

"When is it going to be?"

"Tonight."

"What time?"

"We'll see."

"Nobody is to know about this business of ours."

"Don't worry."

"What kind of a plan . . . ?"

"We'll get him out by telling him they have knocked down the cross again."

"Will he come?"

"He will."

"What if he doesn't?"

"Then we'll do it in the house."

"You alone?"

"No, several of us."

"Can you tell me who?"

"We'll see. I'll get them drunk."

"That's up to you. I don't know a thing. I'll be sleeping."

"Couldn't you let me have something for expenses?"

"Expenses?"

"Yes, at the tavern. I've told El Moro that today the drinks are all on me. With the streets full of drunks, nobody can suspect anybody. And the women will keep quiet for fear it may have been their husband or brother."

"It sounds good to me."

"But . . . wine costs money."

"How much do you want?"

"Give me five hundred more."

"There you are. Anything else?"

"No, that's all."

"Just a little warning. If one word gets around in the village about this arrangement of ours, you can kiss yourself good-by. Is that clear?"

"Perfectly clear. Don't worry."

"Good night."

"Good night."

If Lucio had not been in such a hurry to get away he would have noticed a shadow crouching beside a window. But it was almost invisible, for night had closed in. The clock was just striking ten.

"Come in."

The figure of María the martyr was silhouetted in the doorway. Renato could not see her eyes, but the current of her anger reached him. When she saw María Belén, she screamed at her: "What are you doing here? You go home."

The child lowered her head and went out without saying a word. María moved toward Renato and he could see that her eyes were like those of a wounded lioness. But anyone observing the scene would have noticed that her words seemed to freeze on her lips. Perhaps she felt that wave of peace which many had experienced near Renato. Nobody in the village understood why, but the fact remained that in his presence all reacted differently than they had expected. They felt themselves conquered when beside him, whereas he felt himself defeated by any one of them. Those who managed to hate him had to do it from a distance, because near him they became utterly disconcerted.

Thus, María sat down beside him without making up her mind to speak. She needed to talk, but when she went to open her lips, she had the feeling that her words would be useless. He seemed to have forgotten that she was there, and had buried his head in his hands again, remaining completely motionless.

At last María decided to talk. "Renato."

He raised his head and looked at her as though from a great distance, as though it was an effort for him to return to the world.

"They are going to kill you." She stopped because he had not moved a muscle and gave the impression that he had not heard her. But when she noticed that his jaw grew hard and that his eyes began to clear, she added: "Tonight."

He ran his hand over his forehead. Then he let his head fall back until it rested against the wall. He took a deep breath, almost like a groan. Then he looked at her. Her face revealed utter weariness and an appeal for help. He got heavily to his feet. He went over to the window and rubbed his sleeve across the glass to clear away the dust. He rested his forehead against it. The earth was dark, and all that could be distinguished was several still-darker spots in the background. Suddenly Renato turned. "Go!"

He said this in a tone at once commanding and supplicating. María would have liked to ask him something, but she did not dare, and went out without adding a word. As she closed the door, she remembered that her husband had told her that he wanted to go to bed early that night.

The tavern was unusually quiet. There were as many people as usual, but it was as though they mistrusted one another. El Moro had announced that the drinks were free, but his words had aroused no enthusiasm. He had filled and refilled the glasses; the drinking had been heavy —but that evening even the drunkenness was quiet. Lucio sat in a corner shuffling the faces of those present. He and three more would be enough, he thought. Mentally he chose Santos, Julián, and Martín. Santos and Julián were sitting together at a table. He went over to them.

"I want to talk to you."

Santos looked him up and down slowly, finished his drink, and exchanged glances with Julián. "What about?"

Lucio grimaced a smile and snapped his fingers. "Business."

Santos and Julián exchanged glances again. Santos filled up his glass. Julián smiled. Santos pointed to a chair. "Have a seat."

Lucio gave a sigh of relief. He turned to El Moro. "Bring a bottle of cognac. And four glasses."

"I told you I wanted to go to bed early. Did you forget?"

María said nothing. She felt a repulsion that she could not control rising in her throat. She was fully aware of what was behind all this. She noticed Sátrapa's forced gaiety. While she was getting supper, she heard Don César go to the door and stand chatting with the butcher who was sitting at the window across the way reading the newspa-

227

per. She heard him say that he was very tired and was going to bed early. María knew that what he was doing was impressing everyone with the fact that he was sleeping at home that night. And he chose the moment when Manuela and the twins were coming down the street to take his leave of the butcher and exchange a few words with them at the door of his house. Then he closed it with a bang that all of them could hear.

María could hardly swallow a mouthful that night. Neither could Sátrapa, though she observed his efforts to seem normal. Mealtime was silent, except for one incident.

Dessert had just been set on the table when María saw César turn pale and shout: "A roach!"

He jumped up from the table, knocking over a chair, and ran to the corner between the pantry and the dining-room and began stamping with fury. "You know I can't stand roaches."

María was startled by his violent anger. She knew that he hated insects of any sort, but she had never seen him in such a state.

He sat down and tried to act natural. On the red tiles there was the dark stain of a squashed roach.

Renato still stood with his head resting against the window. A feeling of rebellion was gathering in him, and he made an effort to control it, but his sense of inner emptiness was growing. Nothing around him had meaning. But does anything in this world have meaning?

The night was tense, silent, and deserted. Did anything have meaning? Why the millions of stars? Why man?

The thought that he had been trying to elude wormed its way into his head: what if He does not exist? He was as frightened as if the ground he stood on had given way under him, and his body was filled with tearless weeping. He shook his head as though trying to drive off a persistent fly, but the idea came back in a hundred different guises: "If He exists, how can He stand the world?" It was not man's suffering that frightened him. What horrified him was that of God. That was the only problem. He became aware of the fact that the compassion he had felt for people was beginning to turn to hate. "If I were God . . ." he said. And suddenly it seemed to him that the night had become completely black.

When it struck eleven, a number of glasses were drained in the tavern and some of those present started for the door. Nobody felt like talking, and on every forehead a deep wrinkle evidenced a troubled heart.

As Martín was going out, Lucio called to him: "There's an empty glass here. How about it?"

Martín looked from one to the other. A bond had been established among the three at the table without a word having been spoken as yet. They met Martín's glance with a spark of irony in their eyes. Martín looked around and saw that only they and El Moro were left in the tavern. When he turned his head again, Lucio's expression had become still more ironic.

"Of course, if you don't want to, that will be one less when the time comes to . . ."

But Martín already had sat down.

"Fine. I'm glad I'm not dealing with fools. It makes everything easier," Lucio said.

"My dear . . ."

María looked at him without understanding what he was

after with all that show of affection. For some time he had been smiling that forced smile accompanied by words that she found disgusting. He had come up behind her. And when he laid his hands on her shoulders, she had to make an effort not to stiffen.

"My dear . . ."

Her first impulse was to turn and slap him, to ask him why he did not go to his . . . She forced a smile.

He stroked her neck. "You mustn't neglect your hubby."

It was revolting. He had been putting on flesh, his color was high, and the expression on his full lips grew more sensual every day. His little eyes were glittering with a look of utter stupidity.

"How about a little . . ." He could not finish the phrase. He was doing his best to make the words seem natural. She realized that the supreme sacrifice was being demanded of her. It was indispensable for Sátrapa to have somebody with him when the shots were fired, in case the matter should ever come to trial. And Matilde would not do.

María went into his room as though going to the stake.

Renato shook his head violently and said: "No, not that. I've had enough."

(He was already there. *A cigarette was dangling from the left corner of his mouth, and a smile flickered in his eyes. Renato recognized him immediately in spite of his appearance. At first sight anyone would have mistaken him for some insignificant office worker—the worn gray suit, the carelessly knotted tie, the top button of his shirt unfastened. The hands were well shaped, and even had an air* of elegance. When he took the cigarette out of his mouth a complacent smile showed . . .

"Well, it's nice to meet somebody who's not scared to see me. The ridiculous way the others act, running, screaming. Nonsense! Childish nonsense which I can't understand. Don't they believe in me? Then why are they so surprised when I appear? And they can't put the blame on my get-up. I always use this now. Men have lost their imagination, and if I were to appear with cloven hoofs they'd be capable of sending me to the zoo."

Renato's expression was steadily growing harder.

"Come, now, don't act like that! We're going to be good friends. Isn't it true that you have just used my words? Oh, yes, think back. You said: 'No, not that.' You are now another rebel, exactly like myself. You humans complain loudly about me, but at the hour of the truth you are all mine. God gauges your strength badly. He asks too much of you: saintliness, death . . . Those are big words. I ask reasonable things: vulgarity, stupidity, taking things as they come. That's my program. Now I don't even ask for big sins. Men commit them without my having to tempt them. It comes out much cheaper for me to freeze their souls with idiocy.

"And don't think for a minute I don't hate to give up my old methods. There are times when I have to relinquish my own personality. They said that all this stuff about the devil was too terrible, and so now I use more fashionable terms: tolerance, being up-to-date . . . As you see, it's all very chic. And it works. They are all mine. You too. You said: No. And now you are going to be proud enough not to retract. A real man.

"To tell you the truth, God is aging and He's beginning

231

to get a little senile. In the last analysis, what does He offer you? A sugar-water sky and a few rose-colored statues on repulsive taffy altars. It's not worth going to so much trouble for that.

"I am more understanding. And not even overambitious. Just listen. Hell is overpopulated, and I have hit upon simpler methods. I limit myself to robbing God of the life of His creatures and concern myself less about their death. The priests come: Ascend, ascend, soul, to paradise. The stupid fools! To heaven! An eternity of bliss! What rot! To paradise, to paradise! And they die smiling because in their stupidity they even believe that paradise is the kingdom of balloons. How foolish can they be? Though if God were willing to do business with me, this is what I would propose: a guarantee of heaven for everybody. Then how comfortably everybody could sin! Besides, it would be the way to prove to God what it is that His people want.

"There are those give me a hard time. You, for instance. There was no way to catch you. But, as you see, I have only to wait. Sooner or later comes the word of rebellion. And once it is spoken, there is no taking it back."

The king of lies took a puff of his cigarette and laughed. It was not a guffaw, nor even a sarcastic laugh. It was one of satisfaction, with only a tinge of irony.

"Go away, go away." Renato spoke in a voice that was mild, without anger, but firm and commanding.

"All right, I'll go if you want me to." He laughed again. "Or, rather . . . I will withdraw. For I never go, never." This time his laughter was more prolonged than before. "Especially at this hour. Branches that rustle of themselves —it is I. A knife that glitters in the shadows—it is I. A

232

prayer cut short in the throat—never doubt it for a moment, it is I.

"Sir," and now the tone was frankly ironic, "I shall be waiting for you on the road of our flight together. Get your bags packed, for we are going. See you soon. Good night."

Even after the door had closed, his laughter went on for a few moments. Then silence returned.)

Renato, still shaking his head, said: "I've had enough."

Then he looked around the corners of his room, one by one. He opened a chest and took from it six balls and a few pieces of clothing, lifted down the cross that hung over the bed, and put it all in a sack, which he tied with a string.

He did all this without knowing what he was doing, as though a hand was guiding him. It was the same as the miracles, except that now he had a bitter taste in his mouth.

Then he unhooked the cage of the canary, which awoke frightened and began fluttering against the wires. Renato hesitated for a moment with it in his hand, but finally made up his mind. The night was oppressive, without the least stirring of a breeze.

He raised his eyes. "Forgive me. This is not for me. I will be a good man. That's all."

He stood still for a long time, as though the hand guiding him had suddenly paused. Finally he shook his head. "Find Yourself somebody else."

And he began to walk.

When the glasses were set down on the table, the four looked at each other. They knew exactly what they were

233

going to do, and they hardly needed any further plan than to look into each other's eyes.

Lucio's eyes were small and furtive. They sparkled. There was in them, always, a false smile that gave the impression of a trampled childhood. They were the eyes of a seven-year-old who has just committed his first mortal sin.

Santos's eyes were opaque and gray. Eyes which had seen many things, worn-out eyes. Eyes of a sad animal, a thrashed dog, a thirsty horse.

Martín's was a flayed smile. When one looked into his eyes, one was reminded of a black rock, but when one tried to recall them, what came to mind was the image of a red bonfire, of a blasphemy.

Julián had the look of what he was, a drunkard. His eyes were always bloodshot, but by blood pale in color and repugnant. His mother said that as a child he had looked as though his eyes were smeared with jelly. And it was true.

"Now, can I depend on you to handle him?"

Somebody had called Lucio "mouse-voice," and the nickname fitted him to a tee. Not only because it was a squeaky voice, but because of the combination of timidity and knavery about everything he said. He talked in light squeaks followed by pauses that made it extremely difficult to understand him.

"Any palm-grease?"

Santos nearly always smiled when he talked. But his laugh was false and seemed lost in a sea of sadness. He talked slowly, drawling his words. Martín, on the other hand, talked little and in hammer blows.

"How much?"

Julián's was the muzzy voice of the drunkard. He echoed what others said.

234

"That's right. How much?"

Lucio was frightened as he mentioned the amount. He had always had a great respect for figures.

"Five hundred now. Two thousand afterward. Apiece."

The tavern was thick with smoke, and the air was hard and dense. El Moro had gone into the back room, where he could be heard rattling glasses and bottles. It was pitch dark outside and the sultriness in the air made it hard to breathe.

"Stones are best; they don't have an owner."

"But it would be a good thing to take along a shotgun."

"Good for those that own one."

"I'll get hold of one somehow."

The cognac was now served in big glasses. And the tubercular glow of the light bulb was hectic and bloody.

Sátrapa rolled over on his back. His body was drenched in sweat and his soul in failure. With this went fear. Every time he thought about Renato his whole skin tensed in a shiver like that of fever. As though a frozen mask had been clamped on his body.

María was exhausted. At last it seemed that he was asleep, and she closed her eyes.

Sátrapa shook her violently by the shoulder. "Tell me, were you really resurrected?"

And when he saw that she would not answer, and that two tears welled up in her eyes: "Shut up!" he said, and squeezed her arms brutally. She stopped crying and did not complain.

Renato was walking like an automaton. He was not aware of the oppressive sultriness that made it hard for him to breathe. His whole body was drenched with sweat, but it was as though he did not inhabit his body. A huge moon had now risen, making the night bright. A milky light streamed down on the village. Renato passed the station, but not even then did he realize what he was doing or remember his duties as switchman. What he felt was the urge to flee, but he did not know where. He had set out along the road that led to the highway to León without thinking that he would have to walk miles and miles and that it would be much better to go to Marzales and get the early morning train. Nor did he remember about the five-o'clock train, though he sent it through every day.

Nothing of all this came to his mind. He had taken his things and started to walk. That was all.

As he crossed the track, he stopped for a minute to look at the village. He felt a vague pain that little by little became more concrete. For a moment it seemed to him that the village was picked out in red. He shook his head to drive away the image, but a more horrible one came in its place: he saw a river of blood flowing into the village like a torrent. He covered his eyes with his hands to shut out the vision, but it became clearer every minute. Now he saw with all clarity that the blood was coming from the cross, from its cracks. "I am going mad," he said.

He sat down on a road marker and rested the canary in his lap. The little thing, roused from its sleep, fluttered and gave a pitiful cheep. Renato was not too clear about what the canary was doing there, but, looking at it, he felt more at peace. When he looked at the village again he felt a wave of love rising in him. And tears filled his eyes. "I . . . I . . ." he said.

But this time, too, grief triumphed. He got heavily to his feet, threw the sack over his shoulder, holding it with his right hand, the canary's cage in his left, and made straight for the highway.

The four men approached Renato's house cautiously. They had decided to settle the matter right there. They would throw a stone at the door, and when Renato opened up to see who it was, Santos would fire the shotgun. They had chosen a shotgun because all the hunters in the neighborhood used them. A blast of shot would bring him down. Then they could finish him off with stones. "Stones have no owner," Martín had repeated.

But when the stone hit, the door moved, creaking on its hinges, and the four realized that it was unlocked. They waited a few minutes, just in case. Then Lucio approached cautiously and pushed the door open. Nothing moved inside.

"The bird has flown the coop."

The four looked at one another in perplexity. Martín let out a curse.

It was then that Renato stopped. It was as if a hand were pulling him back. "Someone has cursed," he thought. He turned his head, sure of finding someone. But the road was deserted, the silence absolute. Again he rubbed his forehead. But suddenly he "knew" what he had decided. He could not have explained how, but he could not doubt that a decision had been reached. He took a few more steps along the road, but with the certainty that he would retrace them at once.

And so it was. He did not dare confess to himself the reasons for his return, and he quieted himself by thinking: "I'll just say good-by to the cross, and then I'll go at once." And he added, trying to convince himself: "I couldn't leave without telling it good-by."

237

"So what do we do?"

"What is there to do but go home?"

"I'm almost sorry."

"I'm not. This is lots easier."

"I'm sorry not to collect the rest of the money."

As Renato approached the cross he saw that it was not alone: a strange object was joined to it. As he came nearer he realized that it was someone clinging to the stone. He recalled the drunkard on the day the "whole thing" had begun.

"What are you doing there?"

It was María Belén. The girl let go of the cross without showing the least fright. As though she had been there by appointment. The moonlight revealed her smile, that angelic smile hidden behind her deformed body.

Renato felt suddenly happy. He scolded her, smiling. "It's one o'clock in the morning."

The girl did not answer. She sat down on the upper step, Renato on the lower. She said: "You know, I dreamed they had thrown down the cross again."

Renato looked at her, trying to divine the purpose of her words. But the clear eyes showed only determination.

"I came to defend it."

Renato wanted to ask her who was going to throw down the cross, but for a moment he was afraid that she would answer that it was he, with his running away. He felt that the little lame girl must know his weakness. To put aside the idea, he tried to talk of something else, to ask her how she had managed to slip out of her house. But before he could ask her, the girl had answered: "Tonight I didn't sleep with Mama."

238

Renato trembled. The sap was rising in his heart again. He drew the girl's face down to his and kissed her on the forehead. "Thanks," he said.

"For what?"

The girl had said the words automatically, not really as a question, but as though assuming there was something to give thanks for. Off the Colina de las Angustias a cool breeze began to blow.

"Didn't you see a shadow move there by the cross?"

It was they.

"Listen to me, María Belén. You be good. Be good. When all this is over and you are older and all that is left in you of all this is a faint memory . . . love Him sometime in my name."

"Love God?"

"Yes, God. Love Him. Do you understand?"

The child said nothing, but shook her head affirmatively.

"Now, don't fire unless you have to. Is that clear?"

"It is."

"And if they talk about me, tell them that I loved them."

María Belén raised her hand, and with the index finger of her right hand wiped a tear from Renato's cheek. He picked her up and set her down behind the cross.

"You stay down there so they won't hurt you. And now promise me that you won't say a word about what you're going to see."

The child nodded her head in promise. Renato kissed her again on the forehead, and moved away. But then he came back. "I'm giving you back your canary. Love it."

239

Then María Belén saw him move away from the cross in the direction of the cemetery. She saw him stop. Several shadows came up to him. She heard a cry.

"Keep still."

María Belén's heart was beating fast. She heard a dry thud, as though from a fist. Something struck metal, probably the cemetery gate. María Belén threw her arms around the cross. And then came the terrible blow. She had seen two arms lift a stone as big as a man's head. Then she heard other similar blows, and then there was silence.

Sátrapa felt his limbs contract. His mouth and eyes opened in an expression of horror.

María looked at him. "What have you done?"

"It wasn't me." He said this with a groan like a frightened child, and clung to his wife's body. He was shivering.

María Belén saw the shadows move away. She pressed herself against the cross and wept inconsolably.

But she stopped when suddenly two shots echoed from the end of the street.

❖❖❖❖❖❖❖❖❖❖

21   If it had not been for the two shots Julián fired in his drunkenness, the whole village would have slept better. Or—who knows? —perhaps even without them many would have found it impossible to sleep. Perhaps horror is easier to bear than

uncertainty. Now everything had happened, and the obligation to impede the crime had been lifted from all shoulders, for it was now too late. Who can stop death once it has accomplished its objective?

For that reason many breathed deeply in their beds. They listened attently to find out if anything more was going to happen. But after the two shots there came the longest silence. Then slowly several windows were opened, almost soundlessly.

"Can you see anything?"

All sensed shadows spying like themselves in the window across the way.

"Not a thing."

Suddenly—why?—the woman began to cry. The man grew nervous.

"Now what's the matter?"

The woman gulped down a sob. "He was good."

The man muttered unintelligible words between his teeth. Then the windows closed one by one. The woman shivered in bed.

"Why are you shivering now?"

"I'm afraid."

"Afraid of what?"

"I don't know. Afraid."

The woman became quiet. But then she went on: "Afraid God will punish us."

For she knew only too well the reason for her fear.

The men were afraid to contradict them. All they said was: "Keep quiet."

And they tried to get to sleep, knowing it was impossible.

Neither did the engineer nor the fireman of the express sleep. Nor those of the mixed train. But that was part of their job. A job, if the truth be told, which they did not care much about. To be sure, in summer the night trip was pleasanter because the heat of the sun was not added to that of the firebox. And in winter the heat of the engine kept them warm by day and by night. But, in any case, working at night and sleeping by day was always a bore, especially for the engineer and fireman of the express, who were single and found fewer amusements by day than at night. The night trip annoyed the crew of the mixed train, too, for their wives—both of them were married—complained about that topsy-turvy way of living.

But by this time the four of them had become accustomed to living in this different way from other people, and they did not think about it any more. They had even developed a fondness for the nocturnal landscape, and knew it as well as if they were seeing it by daylight. The men on the express knew that as they pulled out of Irola at two A.M. the Morales lights would be on, and that at four all would be dark at Pedrosa. They knew that about a quarter of five they would pass the mixed train between Marzales and Torre, and that a little after that the switchman of Torre would shunt them onto the single track, after which there would be no other crossing on the road to Portugal. The crew of the mixed train followed the same procedure, but in reverse.

It was a night like any other night, and the conversation at half past four was the same as usual.

"Tell me about this new girl," the express engineer said.

"She's short, dark, with eyes and a figure . . ." The fireman gave an admiring whistle.

"How did you meet her?"

242

"I winked at her and she laughed. Then I said: 'What will you have, baby?' And she said: 'That depends on what is expected of me.' And I said: 'Suppose the sky was the limit?' And she played dumb and said: 'Then make it cognac, and the right brand.' "

"Oh, boy! But then she softened up, I suppose."

"I tell you Madrid will finally bring in that Kopa," the engineer of the mixed train said.

"If I was the National Committee, I'd throw them out," the fireman said.

"You can talk all you like, but the foreigners pack them in. Look at that Di Stefano."

"And then Bilbao wins the championship. With home talent."

The two trains were coming closer in the night. The air was still, as though waiting for something. If the crew of the mixed train had not been so absorbed in their conversation, they would have realized that they had not received their signal.

At twenty of five the fireman of the express said: "Oh, sure, in the end they all lay it on the line."

"I'd like to know how it is you get them to come around so easily."

"Whenever you like, I'll introduce her to you."

"But I like to watch them. When did you ever see anyone from Bilbao who played like Kubala? And if you could have seen the celebration for Molowny," the engineer of the mixed train said.

"With the millions they make, they can afford it."

.　.　.

At eighteen minutes of five the two trains were approaching over the empty plain. The express coaches were almost full. The passengers' eyes had that dull glaze which comes from a night of trying to sleep without being able to. The mixed train was practically empty. In the first car a peasant woman was nursing a six-month infant and trying to put a four-year-old to sleep. "We're almost there, darling."

"It burns me up to see those fellows line their pockets with money while we break our backs for a thousand lousy pesetas. . . ."
"We're the ones that pay to see them."

"Sure, I don't blame you for not wanting to get married. You have your fun and you don't have to feed them."
"Oh, I feed them, all right; what I don't want is a bunch of brats hanging to my coat tail."

By a quarter of five the silence was drawn tight and the rumble of the trains was the only sound in the night.
"There comes the express," said the engineer of the mixed train.
"Yes, today we're early."
"Yes, we almost never pass it before the curve."
At fourteen minutes of five the engineer of the mixed train moved his lever on the curve.
At thirteen minutes of five the engineer of the express said: "Why the hell are you throwing on the brake?"
At thirteen minutes of five the engineer of the mixed train asked: "Did you throw on the brake?"

244

Nobody had put on the brakes, but the two trains were slowing down. When the engineer of the express stuck his head out of the window, he saw the mixed train standing still some twenty yards away. On the same track. When the engineer of the mixed train stuck his head out of the window, he saw the express halted some twenty yards away. On the same track.

The four men got down and walked toward each other. They hardly dared talk. Their blood was frozen in their veins and the faces of the four of them were dripping sweat.

At a quarter of five Renato's name was on the lips of every inhabitant of Torre. It was plain that nobody was going to sleep that night. People talked through half-open doors, and the women hurried softly from one house to another. Nobody knew exactly what had happened, but everything was being whispered about. There was not a conversation in which the word "resurrected" was not heard. Someone had seen Renato walking through the streets of the village, his body enveloped in an almost phosphorescent glow and the smile of a victor on his lips.

All the windows in the village were closed. But behind each the presence of a woman could be sensed, her ear alert for the least rumor. The men were in bed, and made no answer to the questions asked by their wives from time to time.

Outside it was growing lighter. The sun would soon be coming up. But not for this were the doors of the village opened. On the contrary, it seemed as though the wall of silence grew tighter and tighter around each house with the fear that clutched at each throat.

By six in the morning only two words were left in the village: "Dear God, dear God!"

And tears were finished, too. All eyes were dry, finally sterile.

Not even María Belén could cry any more. She had been doing this for five hours. She knelt beside the fallen body, mechanically stroking the bloody hair. The head had been crushed, the inside of the skull laid bare. But the face was unmarred. Only from the tear ducts and the mouth had flowed blood that was now dry and bright red.

"Resurrect, you must resurrect . . ." The child talked as though in her sleep, without realizing what she was saying. ". . . so we can kill you again!"

The morning breeze was blowing, and at any moment the sun would be coming up behind the Colina de las Angustias.

"People always have to kill someone, you know. And so, you always . . ."

The earth was dry and of an ocher color. The child's breast was rising and falling in slow pulsation.

Beautiful, red, and solemn among the trees, the sun came up. And it was at this moment that María Belén's breathing stopped. For Renato's face had begun to glow. The dried blood seemed to come alive under the sun's rays. The child got to her feet in terror. Her eyes were dilated with fright, and she covered her mouth with her hands.

And just then in the east a strong, swift wind sprang up and four purple clouds hid the sun's face. They grew and grew until they had covered the whole village. And María Belén took her eyes from Renato's body, and they filled with tears that were not hers; and through the tears came a smile that spread over her whole face as rain began to fall upon the village.

José Luis Martín Descalzo was born in Madridejos (Toledo), Spain, in 1930. He was ordained in Rome in 1953. He began his literary activity in the poetry review *Estría*, forming part of the youthful movement of priest-writers. In 1952 he won the Insula Prize for poetry with *Seven Sonnets of the Dawn*, poems that were included in his book *Fables with God at Their Foundation*. In 1953 his book *Dialogues of Four of the Dead* won the Naranco Prize for a short novel. In 1955 he published *A Priest Confesses to Himself*, a great success both critically and with the public. With *God's Frontier*, his first full-length novel, he won the 1956 Eugenio Nadal Prize.

A NOTE ON THE TYPE

The text of this book was set on the Linotype in JANSON, a recutting made direct from the type cast from matrices long thought to have been made by Anton Janson, a Dutchman who was a practicing type-founder in Leipzig during the years 1668-1687. However, it has been conclusively demonstrated that these types are actually the work of Nicholas Kis (1650-1702), a Hungarian who learned his trade most probably from the master Dutch type-founder Dirk Voskens.

The type is an excellent example of the influential and sturdy Dutch types that prevailed in England prior to the development by William Caslon of his own incomparable designs, which he evolved from these Dutch faces. The Dutch in their turn had been influenced by Claude Garamond in France. The general tone of the Janson, however, is darker than Garamond and has a sturdiness and substance quite different from its predecessors.

This book was composed, printed, and bound by H. WOLFF, New York. Paper manufactured by P. H. GLATFELTER COMPANY, Spring Grove, Pa. Typography and binding design by GEORGE SALTER.